THE SEARCH

LEFT BEHIND
>THE KIDS<

Jerry B. Jenkins

Tim LaHaye

WITH CHRIS FABRY

TYNDALE HOUSE PUBLISHERS, INC.
WHEATON, ILLINOIS

Visit Tyndale's exciting Web site at www.tyndale.com

Discover the latest Left Behind news at www.leftbehind.com

Published in association with the literary agency of Alive Communications, Inc., 7680 Goddard Street, Suite 200, Colorado Springs, CO 80920.

Scripture quotations are taken from the *Holy Bible,* New Living Translation, copyright © 1996. Used by permission of Tyndale House Publishers, Inc., Wheaton, Illinois 60189. ALl rights reserved.

Scripture taken from the New King James Version. Copyright © 1979, 1980, 1982 by Thomas Nelson, Inc. Used by permission. All rights reserved.

Edited by Curtis H. C. Lundgren

ISBN 0-8423-4329-6

Printed in the United States of America

08   07   06   05   04   03   02   01
10   9   8   7   6   5   4   3   2

To Ryan

TABLE OF CONTENTS

What's Gone On Before

AFTER the vanishings of millions of people, Judd Thompson Jr. and the other kids living in his house make a decision. First, Lionel Washington puts his faith in Jesus Christ. Then Judd Thompson and Vicki Byrne do the same. Ryan Daley and several others join the Young Tribulation Force to spread truth and fight the raging evil around them.

Now, a year and a half after the vanishings, the future of the Young Trib Force is uncertain. The opening attack of World War III has left the kids bruised and scattered.

While searching for the youngest member, Ryan, Judd discovers the body of Pastor Bruce Barnes. During the frantic moments after the bombing stops, Judd and his friend John search for John's cousin, Mark. Mark,

who is heavily involved in the militia movement, narrowly escapes death.

Vicki and her friend Chaya are at the
hospital when planes fly overhead. After a
harrowing run through the neighborhood,
they discover Chaya's mother has also died
in the bombing of the hospital.

At Judd's house, the grief-stricken kids
consider their future. Ryan is missing and
may be dead. But Lionel Washington won't
listen to their fears. He believes Ryan is alive.

Now the kids must pull together like never
before as they search for the truth about their
young friend.

ONE

The Search Begins

RYAN heard movement in the hospital hallway and scrunched behind Bruce's bed. "I gotta go now," Ryan whispered. Bruce wasn't moving anymore. "You get some rest. I'll tell everybody you said hi."

Ryan squeezed Bruce's hand. Bruce didn't respond.

Ryan tiptoed to the stairwell door without being noticed. He closed it gently and bolted down the stairs. When he came out on the first floor, he ducked into the gift shop and bought licorice and a candy bar. He slipped past the older woman at the desk and calmly walked out the emergency-room doors.

Outside, three women were smoking. For a moment, Ryan couldn't get his bearings. Had he come from the right or left?

"Which way to Kirchoff Road?" Ryan said.

A frail woman tried to speak but coughed violently. She pointed to the right.

"Thanks," Ryan said, and he was off.

It felt good to be on his bike again and heading home. Ryan wanted to tell Judd about his visit with Bruce. He knew Judd would be ticked, but he didn't care. Ryan would just laugh and take Phoenix for a run in the park.

As he rode toward a hill, he heard a plane overhead. It was flying low. Too low. Ryan looked up in time to see the underside of the fighter jet. The roar was deafening. Ryan was sure it was going to crash.

He glanced down just as his front tire hit the curb. Ryan struggled to stay up and swerved into the street. Just as he gained control, an earth-shattering explosion behind him threw him to the pavement. His bike skittered ahead. He saw blood on his elbow and a huge hole in his jeans.

Tires screeched. A van was sliding toward him! He stared, frozen, as it demolished his bike and stopped within inches of his face.

He smelled gasoline. Fire crackled behind him. Screams filled the air. More planes flew overhead. Another explosion. Then another. The van backed up and tried to get around him, but his bike was caught underneath. Ryan grabbed the front bumper and pulled himself up. The driver was looking back. The man on the passenger side was short with a round face and looked like he needed a shave. Ryan saw something move in the back of the van.

The driver turned and yelled. The other man banged on the window and screamed, "Get outta the way, kid!"

Ryan ran to check his bike. The crumpled handlebars were caught between the back wheel and the bumper. With the explosions and noise around him, his first thought was to run. Find shelter. Get to safety.

But something drew him to the van. He peered through the tinted window. Nothing. He cupped his hand to block the light and was barely able to make out a kid with heavy gray tape over his mouth. Ryan tapped on the window, and the kid turned. *Blindfolded!*

"Get away from there!" the short man yelled as he jumped out and tried to pry the bike loose. "Stupid kid."

Ryan studied the rear license plate, but the short man yelled, "Help me with this!"

Ryan felt the heat from the explosions, and the smoke made it hard to breathe. He yanked the bike loose and watched the short man throw it aside.

"What's wrong with that kid?" Ryan said.

"What kid?"

"The one with the duct tape."

The man looked at him menacingly. "You didn't see nobody, understand?" The man jumped into the van, and it sped off.

Suddenly it stopped and screeched back right at him. He ran to the hill. The van was right behind him as he neared the top. Flames and smoke rose into the air. Before Ryan could see what was on the other side, the van slid to a stop in the grass, and both men jumped out.

"Get him!" the driver yelled. Before Ryan could react, the short man was on him. They threw him into the back of the van. Ryan banged his head on an armrest and lay on the floor. From there he could see only the kid's hands. Riding boots. Long fingernails. *Weird*, Ryan thought.

The men held Ryan down and taped his hands and feet. He kicked and screamed with all his might, but they were too strong. They laid him sideways beneath the seat. "Sorry, kid," the short man said as the van sped away. "Can't take no chances."

"You're king of the double negative," Ryan said, "you know that?"

The man ignored him and wrapped tape around the back of Ryan's head and over his mouth. *Getting this off is really gonna hurt,*

Ryan thought. Before the man tied the blind-fold, Ryan could see only black smoke out the window. He wondered if he would ever see Bruce or his friends again.

The police, as usual, put Lionel on hold. Finally a cop came on and said, "Your friend will show up, okay?"

"You don't understand," Lionel said.

"No, *you* don't understand," the officer interrupted. "World War III just broke out, in case you didn't notice. We got fires, we got people trapped in rubble, looters, more bombs. Now stop buggin' us. Find him your-self."

Lionel wanted to scream.

"Don't call the police again," Judd said. "All we need is them snooping around here."

"We should at least try to find Ryan," Lionel said. "He'd do that for you."

"I wouldn't want him to," Judd said. "That puts everybody in danger."

"Then why'd you go out this morning?" Lionel said. "That put us in danger."

"That was before the bombs started," Judd said.

Vicki and Chaya pleaded with them to

calm down. "We need to pull together," Vicki said.

"I don't even want to survive," Chaya said. "Going to heaven has to be better than living without my mother or Bruce or Ryan."

Lionel crossed his arms and shook his head.

Vicki put a hand on Lionel's shoulder. "We all want to find him," she said. "It's just hard to even think straight."

"He probably went to his stash of Bibles," Lionel said. "He could be there hiding—or the place could have been bombed and he's trapped."

"Does anybody know where he hides them?" Judd said.

"I was with him when he started picking them up," Vicki said, "but he never showed me where he put them."

Judd sat on Lionel's bed and rubbed his face with both hands. "Let's go through this one more time," Judd said. "You're sure Ryan wasn't at the hospital?"

"We didn't see him," Vicki said. "And they don't allow kids in intensive care."

"That's what *I* told him," Judd said. "He thought I was trying to shut him out."

"You were!" Lionel said.

"I was trying to take care of him," Judd said. "Let's back up. Ryan was mad because

6

we didn't let him in on the meeting about Mark."

"So was I," Lionel said.

"He wanted to go see Bruce, and I told him to forget it."

"Yeah, that's when he took off," Lionel said.

"When he came back he brought me a card and asked me to give it to Bruce when I saw him."

"And you said you would, *if you had the chance*," Lionel said. "If you hadn't been so—"

"This is not helping," Judd interrupted.

"What kind of card?" Vicki said.

"Excuse me?" Judd said.

"What kind of a card did Ryan get for Bruce?"

"Why does that matter?" Judd said.

"It was something about heaven," Lionel interrupted, trying to remember. "That's it. He found a card that looked like heaven, and he wanted Bruce to see it."

"What did you do with the card?" Vicki said.

"I left it over there. Hey, it's gone!"

"He *was* there!" Vicki shouted.

"What are you talking about?" Judd said.

"On the nightstand by Bruce's bed there

was this card, blue sky with clouds—like heaven. That has to be Ryan's card. He could have gotten someone else to deliver it, but the nurses and the orderly hadn't seen him, so it only makes sense that he gave it to Bruce himself."

"But how?" Judd said.

"You sell him short," Lionel said. "He's a lot smarter than you think."

Judd hung his head. "He may have been inside when the bomb hit."

"You guys don't know him like I do," Lionel said. "If he saw Bruce, he would have come back here fast. He'd have wanted to tell you, Judd. He'd have been juiced about it."

"Then where is he?"

"I don't know," Lionel said. "That's why we have to go back to the hospital."

More explosions rocked the van when they drove away, but then the bombing stopped. The traffic must have been bad. Ryan felt lots of stops and starts. The men didn't say much, and with the tape over his mouth, Ryan couldn't talk to the other kid.

Every time the van stopped, Ryan slid forward and hit his head on the metal posts under the captain's chair. The short man laughed at him. Ryan finally managed to roll onto his side and position himself so he wouldn't get hurt at every stop. The floor of the van felt filthy.

Ryan tried to pick up sounds, but mostly he heard the hum of traffic. Someone kept punching buttons on the radio. Finally a news station interviewed an eyewitness to the bombings. A flurry of reports about the damage followed. There were chaos and terror throughout the world. New York City had been hit.

"Ah, who cares about New York?" the driver said. "Maybe it'll clear up some traffic."

The short man laughed, and someone turned up the radio.

". . . devastating carnage everywhere in the heart of Manhattan," the reporter said. "Bombed-out buildings, emergency vehicles picking their way through debris, Civil Defense workers pleading with people to stay underground."

Ryan thought of Chloe and Buck. Their apartment was in New York. They had been in Chicago the week before, but could they have gone back before the bombing?

Ryan heard the panic in the reporter's voice. "I'm seeking shelter myself now, probably too late to avoid the effects of radiation. No one knows for certain if the warheads were nuclear, but everyone is being urged to take no risks. Damage estimates will be in the billions of dollars. Loss of life is impossible to determine. . . ."

"You think those bombs we came through were *nuc-u-lar?*" the short man said.

"Shh, I'm trying to hear this," the other man said.

"All major transportation centers have been closed or destroyed," the reporter continued. "Huge traffic jams have snarled the Lincoln Tunnel, the Triborough Bridge, and every major artery out of New York City. What has been known as the capital of the world looks like the set of a disaster movie."

The other kid sniffled throughout the ride. They were speeding when a huge blast shook the earth. The short man cursed. "Look at that mushroom cloud!" he shouted.

A few minutes later the Cable News Network/Global Community Network coverage explained the blast. "Our news base in Chicago has been taken out by an incredible explosion. The bomb has flattened O'Hare International Airport. No word yet on whether this was an attack by militia forces or a Global Community retaliatory strike. We have so many reports of warfare, bloodshed, and death in so many major cities around the globe that it will be impossible for us to keep up with all of it."

"What luck," the driver said. "Can you believe this timing? Even if the kid's dad goes to the cops, they'll be so busy, they won't have time to worry about us."

The traffic slowed; then the van took sharp turns. Finally they stopped. Ryan heard a garage door open, then they drove inside. It sounded as if the two men carried the other kid away. Then they came back for Ryan. They cut the tape over his ankles, and he climbed, still blindfolded, three flights of stairs. The place smelled of wood, and boards creaked under his feet. Ryan heard horns, sirens, and a rumbling. *A train,* he thought. He knew from going to Cubs games with his dad that the elevated train snaked through Chicago, and he guessed it was somewhere along the miles of that track that he'd been taken. But he couldn't be sure. He had been in the van an hour and could even be in Wisconsin or Indiana.

Someone pushed him from behind and steered him to a door. He heard a key in a lock and the driver arguing with the other man.

The short man said, "You should have just kept going and left him there."

"Too late now," the other man said.

"I could take him to the river or, well, there's a hundred ways to take care of him."

"Let's keep 'em both for now," the driver said. "Stick him in the utility room."

Someone cut the tape from Ryan's arms and pushed a greasy cheeseburger and some fries into his hands. When the man ripped the tape from Ryan's mouth, it took a patch of hair from his neck, and Ryan yelped.

"There's no easy way to do that," the man said. "Sorry."

He led Ryan into another room and took off his blindfold. The room was dark.

"Keep walking," the man said. "Mattress is on the floor. And you two keep quiet."

Ryan sat, letting his eyes adjust. A thin strip of light sneaked underneath the door. Heavy curtains blocked light from outside. Ryan held his hand in front of his face but could barely see it.

The other kid's voice startled him. He hadn't expected the voice of a girl.

Judd, Lionel, and Vicki hurried back to Northwest Community Hospital through massive traffic jams. Smoke still hung in the air. Emergency crews picked through the rubble looking for survivors. Though there were scores of emergency vehicles and hundreds of people, an eerie silence hung over the search.

Judd explained their situation to a guard.

"Did anyone inside survive?" Vicki said.

"They found a baby," the guard said. "Only others I know of were three women on their smoke break outside. They were taken to Lutheran General."

"Maybe one of them saw Ryan," Lionel said. "Let's go."

TWO

Darrion

RYAN jumped when he heard her.

"Of all the indignities," she said. "It's bad enough being kidnapped by a couple of bumpkins. Now I have to share a room."

He couldn't see her, but her voice was thin and proper. She spoke as if she were drinking a cup of tea with her little finger in the air.

"My name's Ryan," he said.

"Darrion Stahley," she said. "I wish I could say I was pleased to meet you, but under the circumstances, I'm not. Where are we?"

Ryan explained his hunch that they were in Chicago.

"How dreadful. I told my father if he decided to move us to Chicago I wouldn't live anywhere close to the city."

"What's wrong with Chicago?"

"If I have to tell you," she said, "it's not

15

worth the breath. The violence. The dirt. Not to mention the noise." A train passed again, and she paused. "See what I mean?"

"Living in the suburbs didn't protect you from those guys," Ryan said.

"I was riding at the stables. They must have watched me, planned it all along."

That explains the boots, Ryan thought. "Why would they kidnap you?" he said. "Are you rich or something?"

"My father is a powerful man, and yes, he is rich. I'm sure he'll take care of these guys. Until then—" Darrion screamed. "Something's crawling on me! Get it off!"

Ryan banged the mattress. He didn't hit anything, but it seemed to make the girl feel better.

"You stirred up the dust!" she coughed.

"You're welcome," Ryan muttered.

"I can't take this!" Darrion screamed. She kicked at the floor. The short man opened the door a crack, and the light allowed Ryan to see Darrion's face for the first time. She was pretty. She was small with short, brown hair. That's why he had thought she was a boy.

"We need light," Darrion demanded. "The room is filled with little creatures scurrying about. If you have to leave us in such deplorable conditions, the least you could do is give us light so we can stay out of their way."

The short man remained behind the door, out of sight, but Ryan could see his shadow. The man shook his head. "Shut up, kid," he said, and closed the door.

"You don't understand," the girl shouted. "My father won't like this!"

Ryan heard the men laugh. Then the light at the bottom of the door went out.

"Nice try," Ryan said, moving toward the wall.

"You think you can do better?" Darrion said.

"Yeah, I think I can."

"I'd like to see you try," she said.

Ryan felt along the wall, then stood. "Why didn't you tell me you wanted some light?" He switched on a flashlight and pointed the beam to her face.

"Where'd you get it?"

"I saw it when the guy opened the door. They must have put it down when they brought you in and forgot about it."

Ryan handed the flashlight to Darrion. She shone it in his face. "What did you say your name was?"

"Ryan," he said, squinting in the light.

"Ryan Daley. What kind of a name is Darrion?"

"What's wrong with it?" she said.

"Nothing, it's just unusual."

"Take that up with my parents," she said. "So, what happened today, with the explosions and everything?"

"Beats me," he said. "A bunch of planes went over and the bombs started dropping."

"I wonder if they've called my father yet," Darrion said, ignoring Ryan. "He'll be worried, I'm sure. My mother as well."

"Yeah," Ryan said.

Darrion scanned the room with the light. Old mattresses lined three of the walls almost to the ceiling. Ryan saw bugs scurry into cracks in the corner.

"I hope they come for me before nightfall. There's no way I'll be able to sleep in a place like this."

"How old are you?" Ryan said.

"Almost fourteen," Darrion said.

"Wow, same here."

"Whoop-de-doo," Darrion said. "We're the same age and being held hostage in a padded cell." She rolled her eyes. "I'm hungry. The food they brought was disgusting."

"You don't like cheeseburgers?"

"I'm a vegetarian. The only thing close to

edible on the plate was the lettuce, and it was dripping with grease."

"You never eat meat?" Ryan said.

"The thought of eating a cow isn't appetizing to me, is it to you?"

"Well, no, but—"

"That's exactly what you did. Animals and people are the same. We're just a little higher up the food chain. Just because I have the ability to speak doesn't give me the right to eat something that doesn't."

"Yeah, well, I still like cheeseburgers," Ryan said, digging into his pocket. Darrion snatched the licorice from his hands.

"Vegetarians eat licorice?" Ryan said, opening the candy bar.

"Low fat," Darrion said.

Lutheran General Hospital was packed with injured people and their families. Vicki and Lionel paced while Judd went to the front desk. He came back dejected.

"They won't tell me anything," Judd said.

Vicki stopped an orderly and asked where the Northwest Community survivors were.

"Are you Dorothy's daughter?" the orderly said. "Your mom's real worried that you'd think she was dead. She's up on the third floor, but you can't go in there."

Vicki thanked her. "I'll go talk with her," she said to Judd and Lionel.

"How you gonna do that?" Judd said.

Vicki grabbed a volunteer's smock from a coatrack and walked toward the elevator. Judd and Lionel gave her a thumbs-up as the doors closed.

Dorothy had fallen as she tried to run from the bombs. She was frail with leathery skin. Her hair was thin, and she coughed violently during the conversation. Even when she wasn't talking, she wheezed through tired lungs.

Vicki fluffed her pillow and tried to make her feel more comfortable. "They said you came over from Northwest Community," Vicki said.

"I'm in the cancer ward," the woman said.

"I have a friend who was over there this morning," Vicki said, "a boy about thirteen or fourteen, riding a bike—"

"A blond kid?" Dorothy interrupted.

"Yes!" Vicki said. "What happened?"

"He asked directions. A couple minutes before the explosion."

"Directions where?" Vicki said.

Dorothy rubbed her head. "He was looking for Kirchoff Road. Seemed like he couldn't get his bearings. He took off up the hill. That's the last I saw of him."

Ryan kept the flashlight off to save the battery. He inspected the windows and felt along the wall behind the mattresses.

"What are you doing?" Darrion said.

"Trying to find a way out," Ryan said.

"I already checked."

Ryan scratched at the windows to let some light through.

"It's painted on the outside," Darrion said.

"Wait a minute," Ryan said excitedly. He pulled out his wrist messenger.

"What?" Darrion said, grabbing for the flashlight.

"Our shot at getting out of here," Ryan said. "I can get in touch with my friends using this thing. Douse the light."

Ryan fiddled with the gadget and frowned.

"What's wrong?" Darrion said.

"Smashed. Must have happened when I fell."

"Wait till my father comes," Darrion said. "He'll get us out of here."

"He may get *you* out," Ryan said. "Did you get a look at their faces?"

"They wore masks."

"I saw both of them—and their van."

"So?"

"They don't dare release me," Ryan said. "I could identify them."

Judd swung by the house and picked up Phoenix. They took him to the hill above the hospital.

Lionel held one of Ryan's shirts, and Phoenix sniffed it excitedly. Judd and Vicki watched as the dog yanked Lionel toward the yellow police tape surrounding the rescue site.

"Ryan was here," Judd said. "Get Phoenix to turn around."

Lionel tried to drag Phoenix from the tape, but the dog barked and raised up on his hind legs, straining against the leash. Vicki held out Ryan's shirt and got Phoenix back on the trail.

They reached the top and continued down the other side of the hill. Phoenix led them to the middle of a residential street. Bits of broken plastic lay on the ground.

"There are marks on the road back here too," Lionel said. "Like somebody slammed on their brakes."

"That could have happened anytime, couldn't it?" Vicki said.

Phoenix was off before Lionel could respond, zigzagging from the road to the curb and back to the middle of the street. Vicki yelped, and Judd found her on the ground.

"I tripped over that thing," Vicki said.

Judd's heart sank when he saw the twisted piece of metal that had been Ryan's bike. Phoenix barked and strained even more when he caught scent of the bicycle.

"What are you going to do?" Darrion said.

"Pray," Ryan said.

"No, really."

"I'm serious," Ryan said.

"Look, if you're right, you're in real trouble here. You need a plan."

Judd's cell phone rang as they returned to the car. Lionel answered.

"Lionel, it's John. I've been calling hospitals since you guys left. Mark and I finally logged on and accessed admission logs. I think I found him."

"Where?" Lionel said.

"Lutheran General."

"We were just there and talked to a lady who saw him before the bombing."

"The kid on the list is pretty banged up, but he fits the description. Unidentified teenager, blond."

Lionel, Judd, and Vicki sped to the emergency room and said they might be able to identify an injured teen. They were directed to a long corridor filled with anxious family members.

"We have three unidentified kids who are thirteen or fourteen," an attendant said. "The only boy was unconscious when they brought him in."

"Can we see him?" Judd said.

"Let me check," the woman said.

A few minutes later she returned with a grim face. "I'm sorry," she said. "The boy died. Can you identify him, help us contact his family?"

"We are his family," Lionel said. "His mom and dad are dead."

"Just one of you, please."

"Can you handle it?" Judd said.

Lionel waited in the hallway outside the morgue while they retrieved the body. His stomach was in knots. He thought about Ryan and how they had fought. The little guy wasn't so little anymore. He was annoying at times, got on Lionel's nerves. But Lionel wished he had another chance.

Lionel was led into a cold, sterile room. A sheet covered the body on a metal table.

"Are you okay?" the man said.

"Wait," Lionel said, then took a deep breath. He nodded and closed his eyes as the man lifted the sheet.

Lionel opened his eyes, and a wave of emotion swept over him. The boy on the table had been badly burned, but this wasn't his friend.

"He could have been taken to some other hospital," Lionel told the others. "Don't they sometimes fly 'em by helicopter downtown?"

"It's worth a shot," Judd said. "John can check that out while we follow leads here."

"What leads?" Vicki said.

"We're assuming he was hurt," Judd said. "Let's assume he didn't get hurt."

"Maybe somebody in the neighborhood helped him," Vicki said.

"He would have called us," Lionel said.

Ryan heard a cell phone ring in the other room. He crawled to the door and strained to hear.

"Yeah, boss," the driver said, "she's fine. No, the timing was perfect. We took off with her, and then all those bombs went off. No sir, she didn't see either of us."

Ryan heard the short man whispering to the driver, "Tell him about the other kid."

"No, we didn't see any family members or workers." The man paused. "No, we did just like you said. We haven't made contact with anybody."

The driver was pacing as he talked.

"Tell him about the other kid!" the short man badgered.

"Yes, sir," the driver said. "We understand. She won't be harmed unless you give the word."

The driver hung up, and the short man exploded. "I can't believe you didn't tell him! What's he gonna do when he finds out we got two kids instead of one?"

"He doesn't need to know," the driver said.

"He won't pay us, that's what he'll do!"

"Listen, by the time they're ready to release the girl, we'll have taken care of the other kid."

The two went into another room. Ryan wondered what "taken care of" meant. He went back to the mattress on the floor. Darrion was right. He needed a plan. And fast.

Vicki felt drained. Bruce, the man who had helped change her life, was gone. Her friend Chaya had lost her mother in the bombing. Another Young Tribulation Force member, Mark, had nearly been killed, and where was Ryan? Vicki was hanging by a thread, but there wasn't time to think about that now.

Judd was taking them, along with Phoenix, back to the road where they had found Ryan's crumpled bike. Lionel had been on the cell phone with John.

"John can't find any kids transported by helicopter or anyone fitting Ryan's description."

"It's crazy right now," Vicki said. "The records are probably incomplete. People aren't concerned with keeping record of the dead. They want to help the living."

Lionel looked hard at Vicki. "He's not dead," he said. "Stop talking that way."

Phoenix picked up the trail from the road and took them through tall grass near the hill overlooking Northwest Community Hospital. As they neared the top, Lionel shouted, "Look at these tracks!"

In the grass, Vicki saw two sets of deep tire marks.

Phoenix came back to the tracks and barked. He sniffed through the area and whined, tipping his head this way and that.

"I'm no bloodhound," Judd said, "but this is where Ryan's trail ends."

"So maybe the bombs caused a car to swerve and knock Ryan off his bike," Vicki said. "Then, whoever was in the car helped him."

"Maybe he didn't get hit at all," Lionel said. "What if he was off his bike? The person in the car gave him a ride because the thing was smashed."

"Then why haven't we seen him or heard from him?" Judd said. "We either find Ryan or we find somebody who saw what happened."

THREE

Clue Quest

*RYAN hurdled the toppled trash bin and flew
down the alley. He wanted to stop and catch his
breath, but he knew he had to keep running. It
was his only chance.*

He heard the screech of tires. A car flattened a trash bin like a pop can. Ryan kept
moving. He passed houses with gang
symbols spray painted on the outside.

He jumped the turnstiles of the elevated
train. The cashier screamed at him. Ryan
shouted back, "Call the police!"

"I'll call them on you!" the cashier said.

His legs were lead as he ran up the stairs. A
pay phone. Call Judd, *he thought. No money in
his pockets. He didn't have time anyway. Two
doors slammed, and the men were gaining on
him.*

People milled about, waiting for the next

train. A businessman with his nose in the paper. A woman with a frilly dress and tennis shoes. Ryan ran through the crowd to a chain-link fence at the end of the platform. Trapped! The only way out was to run onto the tracks.

He jumped.

A woman screamed, "No!"

He wasn't trying to kill himself. He wanted to live. So he kept running, staying away from the dangerous third rail. One misstep, and he was dead.

He saw the men jump onto the tracks. Then he heard a noise. Felt it. It started as a low rumbling, like the vibration of speakers on his stereo. He looked up to see the train a hundred yards away and coming fast. He turned, but the men were close now. He ran toward the oncoming train.

Finally, the men retreated. The train blew its horn. Even if the conductor slammed on the brakes, Ryan knew it would be too late. He had to jump the third rail.

The woman screamed again. She was behind the men. It looked like . . . but it couldn't be.

"Mom?" Ryan said, the train bearing down on him. His foot wedged in the track. The sound was deafening.

"Ryan, jump!" the woman screamed.

Ryan sat up in a sweat.

The sound of the elevated train rumbled outside the window. He shuddered and wiped his brow with his shirtsleeve. He was sore from his bike accident. He flipped on the flashlight and saw Darrion sitting on her bed with her legs crossed underneath her.

"Lunch made you a little drowsy, huh?" Darrion said. "What's wrong?"

"Bad dream," Ryan said. "What're you doing?"

"Meditation," she said. "Gets me in touch with myself and my surroundings. So what scared you?"

"I don't want to talk about it."

"Come on," she said, "dreams tell us a lot about ourselves. A window to the soul and all that. My parents let me go to a psychic once. I told her what I'd dreamed, and she said my life was going to be filled with tranquility."

Ryan raised an eyebrow and looked around the room.

"So what's your plan?" she said quickly.

"I have to get out of here," Ryan said, "but first I have to encourage our friends in the next room to let me stay alive."

"I'll demand they not harm you."

"Yeah, that'll work. They wouldn't even give you a lightbulb."

While Lionel and Vicki took the other side of the street, Judd set off alone. He went from house to house asking if anyone had seen Ryan. Chaya called on his cell phone.

"You just got an E-mail from Nina in Israel," Chaya said. "She saw the reports about the war and wanted to make sure you were okay."

"What about over there?" Judd said.

"Didn't say. I gave her your cell phone number. She was anxious to talk to you. Any luck with Ryan?"

Judd explained what they were doing and urged Chaya to pray. "You doing okay?" he said.

"Yeah," she said. "Looking for Ryan is helping me focus on something else. If I stop to think about what happened today, I'm no help to anyone."

A few minutes later Nina called. Judd told her how close the bombings were and the situation with Ryan.

"I'm so sorry," Nina said. "I will be praying for your friend."

"What's it like there?" Judd said.

"We have seen none of the violence the rest of the world is experiencing," Nina said.

"But the pressure on my father is intense. I have talked with my mother about plans to come to America, and she is open to it. Does the offer still stand?"

"You bet," Judd said, knowing their money troubles were increasing. He pushed the thought away and said, "We'll work it out. You just get here."

"If my father gives the okay, we could be there as soon as next week."

"Great, keep me posted," Judd said.

Vicki and Lionel approached with puzzled looks.

"Nobody's seen anything," Vicki said, "but there's something strange over there." She pointed to a small white house across the street. "The lady who answered the door wouldn't even talk to us. When we went to the next house, we heard a tapping noise coming from inside. The windows are boarded up. It sounded like somebody trying to get out. Creepy."

"Better go back and check it out," Judd said.

As they neared the house they heard a car start, and the garage door opened. The kids scrunched behind a tree.

"That's her," Vicki said, "the one who wouldn't talk to us."

After the woman drove away, Judd rang
the doorbell. There was no answer.

"I know there's somebody in there," Vicki
said.

The three kids went to the side of the
house. Judd peered through a crack in one of
the boards. He saw old furniture covered in
dust. Cats were perched on windowsills
around the room. Suddenly Judd saw a
woman's face.

"Go to the back," the woman said through
the glass.

The woman ushered the kids inside and
said, "You have to be careful. Anna doesn't
like me talking to anyone with all that's
going on."

"What's going on?" Judd said.

"There's evil out there," the woman said.
"First, all those people disappeared. Then
this guy from Romania takes over. Next thing
you know, they're droppin' bombs in your
backyard."

"We're looking for somebody," Judd said,
"a boy on a bike."

"These people hate cats," the woman
continued. "There's a shortage, you know. A
few months ago the shelves were full. Now
there's only a few cans left."

Judd frowned. "What does cat food have to
do with—?"

"It has everything to do with it. They want control. First they start with the little animals, then they come for the children. It's already started."

Judd turned to leave.

"Wait," Lionel said. "What's happening to the children?"

"They're taking the kids away," she said. "Snatching them off the street."

"Did that happen this morning?" Lionel said.

"I can't tell you any more. Anna wouldn't like it."

"Please," Lionel said, "our friend was riding a bike near here. If you saw something, we need your help."

"You know what I think?" the old woman said. "I think the bombs were a diversion. They're taking the kids and brainwashing them so they can have a whole army of little robots."

Vicki picked up one of the cats and stroked it until it purred. "You've been so kind to us," Vicki said, "and you have such beautiful animals. But what we really need to know is if you saw anything."

"When they control the pets—"

"His name is Ryan," Vicki continued, "and he has blond hair. His parents were both killed. We're taking care of him. You can imagine how bad we feel. We thought he was dead, but now we're not sure."

Judd saw a spark in the old woman's eyes. She stared out the window. "My father died when I was ten," she said. "He worked for the electric company. One morning he promised he'd bring me a surprise when he came home. But he didn't make it. . . ."

The old woman wiped her eyes with a paper towel. Vicki put a hand on her shoulder.

"I did see the poor boy," she said. "Anna doesn't like me to go out, but when the bombs went off I stepped onto the porch."

"What did you see?" Vicki said.

"I heard tires squeal and looked down at the curve in the street," she said. "There was a white van. Two men. They'd run over a bicycle and were trying to get it out from under the van. Then they backed up and tried to grab the boy."

"Did they get him?" Judd said.

"Yeah," the old woman said, "they caught him in the grass."

"What happened then?" Vicki said.

"Another bomb went off. I went to the back and saw the smoke and fire. When I looked again, the guys and the kid were gone. I tried to call the police, but Anna said we shouldn't get involved."

"Did you see their license plates?" Judd said.

"Too far away," she said.

Judd opened the back door to leave.

"Thank you for helping us," Vicki said, "and I'm sorry about your father."

The old woman smiled.

Ryan stashed the soda cans under his mattress. "Never know when little things like this might come in handy," he said.

Darrion explained her father's business. "He did a lot of work for the Global Community after the disappearances," she said. "They wanted to promote him, which we thought meant the East Coast. You know, New York, Washington D.C. But he wound up here in the Midwest."

"So your dad works for Nicolae Carpathia?" Ryan said.

Darrion nodded. "He's met him lots of times," she said. "My dad told me about it. He said when Nicolae shakes your hand, you feel like you're the only person in the room. Like you're really important to him. Nicolae remembers everybody's name, you know."

Ryan felt sick inside. That was exactly what

Bruce had said about the Antichrist. He could manipulate people. "Did you lose anybody in the disappearances?" Ryan asked.

"Just an aunt and an uncle," Darrion said. "They were both crazy, though."

"What was wrong with them?" Ryan said.

"Religious wackos," Darrion said. "A few years ago they went over to Europe and got mixed up in some religious group. When they came home, they tried to get my dad to read the Bible and go to church with them."

"And your dad didn't buy it?"

"We've always been religious, open minded. But they were so narrow. If you didn't believe exactly what they did, you were cooked."

"So if they were wrong, what do *you* think about God?"

"I believe in the unity of all living things. God is in us and in all that exists."

"That's why you're a vegetarian."

"Precisely."

"So, when you eat a carrot, aren't you eating God?" The words were out of Ryan's mouth before he could stop them.

"I'm into Enigma Babylon One World Faith," Darrion said, ignoring the comment. "It takes the best of all the belief systems. It's not trying to hurt people like my aunt and uncle were."

"You didn't tell me they hurt you."

"They tried to scare us. You know, they talked about hell. Made God out to be mean."

The men were moving around in the next room. Ryan put a finger to his lips and silently crept to the door.

"If you'd have just kept going, we wouldn't have to—"

"Don't start!" the man said.

"Why do we have to wait till it gets dark?" the short man said. "Let's do it now."

"And how we gonna do it?"

The two men closed the door and went into another room.

"What did they say?" Darrion said.

"Looks like they're gettin' tired of me quicker than I thought," Ryan said. "I'd better come up with something fast."

Ryan prayed silently for an idea. "Please, God, show me how to get out of here. Unless this is where you want me to be. And if it is, open Darrion's heart and let me talk with her about you."

Judd, Vicki, and Lionel regrouped at Judd's house. Judd tried to phone Sergeant Thomas Fogarty of the Chicago Police Department.

Sergeant Fogarty had helped the kids before. The line was busy.

"I just talked with Mrs. Fogarty on the other line," Lionel said. "It's almost impossible to reach the police downtown."

"Tell me about it," Judd said.

"She's gonna have him call us when he gets home or if he gets in touch with her," Lionel said.

"What about the local police?" Judd said. "We should call—"

"Already done. They're just as busy. When I got them to listen to the evidence, they said I should come down and fill out a missing person's report. The cop didn't sound too hopeful that it would do any good."

"Probably won't," Judd said.

Judd and Vicki dropped Lionel off at the police station and swung by New Hope Village Church. Judd found Loretta, Bruce's assistant, red-eyed and sniffling. She was nearly seventy and sitting in the outer office in front of a silent television.

"People been callin'," Loretta said. "I don't know what to tell them. Buck and Chloe Williams came in and told me about Bruce. They didn't actually see him, but Rayford Steele did. I wish I could talk with Ray, just to know Bruce didn't suffer."

Judd knelt by Loretta's chair. "I saw him," he said.

Loretta's face was puffy. "How was he?" she said. "I mean, was his body hurt badly?"

Judd was glad he didn't have to dance around the truth. He had seen Bruce under the white sheet. The sight of his face had taken his breath away, it was true. But when he thought about Bruce's face, Judd smiled.

"He looked like he was sleeping," Judd said. "Peaceful. All those sirens and people crying and running everywhere, and there was Bruce—just like he was when he was alive. Calm."

"That young man was like family to me," Loretta said. "He was my only family. You know my story, don't you?"

"I know a lot of your family members were taken in the Rapture," Judd said.

"I lost everybody," Loretta said. "Every living relative. More than a hundred. I came from a church family. I was one of the leading women in this church. I was active in everything, but I never really knew the Lord."

"That's why Bruce meant so much to you," Judd said.

"That young man taught me everythin'," Loretta continued. "I learned more from him in two years than I learned in more than sixty years in Sunday school and church. There's gonna be an awful big hole in my heart now that Bruce is gone. I'm sorry to go on and on. How are your friends?"

Judd explained the situation with Ryan. "The poor thing," Loretta gasped. "I hope he's okay. He learned so much from Bruce in such a short time. He was like a little sponge."

Judd noticed a huge stack of pages on Loretta's desk in the other room.

"It's Bruce's legacy to the church," Loretta said. "It was Buck Williams's idea. I was feelin' all puny, and he said I could still serve the Lord by serving Bruce. He said just from glancing at those pages that Bruce was still with us. His knowledge, his teaching, his love and compassion are all there."

"So what's Mr. Williams going to do?" Judd said.

"He wants me to help print those pages. He says people in the church need access to the material. It's a treasure everyone can use."

"I watched Bruce write some of that while we were in Israel together," Judd said.

"There's powerful stuff there," Loretta said. "Go ahead. I'm sure Bruce would want you to."

Judd leafed through the pages, and tears came to his eyes. *No wonder Buck Williams wants to get this into the hands of people,* he thought.

FOUR

The Secret Room

WHILE Ryan thought of a plan to save his life, Darrion discussed her horse, her private school, her friends in Italy, and more. Ryan thought he was a privileged kid, but his life was nothing compared to hers. Vacations on islands he'd never heard of. A private jet to carry her anywhere in the world. *Her dad must really be loaded,* Ryan thought.

"I don't understand," Darrion said. "My dad should have given them the money by now."

"These guys are working for someone else," Ryan said. "They didn't call your parents."

"So these guys are just waiting for directions?"

"Looks that way," Ryan said. "And they're making a big deal about the pay. That's why I have to be out of the way. They don't want to threaten their paycheck, which is you."

"Why didn't they just ask my dad for the money themselves?" Darrion said.

"I don't know. It's strange."

Darrion sighed and wilted on the bed. "What could those people want?"

Sergeant Fogarty called, and Judd explained the situation. The officer listened with interest. "Why would anyone want to kidnap your friend?" he said.

"That's what we can't figure out," Judd said.

"You can't be positive it was him," Fogarty said. "Some other kid could have—"

"The witness we found described him," Judd said.

"I believe you," Sergeant Fogarty said. "I'm just trying to think of all the angles."

Sergeant Fogarty said he would try to help, but with the mayhem on the streets, the chances of finding Ryan were slim. Even if they did discover some kind of lead, the officers were swamped with just keeping the peace.

Chaya phoned from the church office. "You guys need to get over here right away," she said.

The men wore masks so Darrion wouldn't
see their faces. They grabbed Ryan and led
him from the room. Darrion barked at the
two, saying her father would be upset if anything happened to Ryan.

"Who says we're going to hurt your
friend?" the short man said. "We're just
gonna take a little ride down by the lake."

"Shut up," the driver said.

They hustled Ryan into the next room and
taped his hands behind him.

"Should we blindfold him?" the short man
said.

"What for?" the driver said.

"Good point," the short man said, snort-
ing. "How about his feet?"

"Let him walk down."

The men shoved Ryan at the top of the
stairs. He lost his balance and fell. He was
groggy as they pulled out of the garage.

On the street Ryan realized his hunch was
right. Chicago. The building they were in was
surrounded by other apartments. He saw the
L tracks and a tiny alley that ran beside them.
Cars were parked along the alley with no
space between them. A block away Ryan
noticed an abandoned factory. Men in old

coats stood by a burning trash can outside. A police car was pulling up as they went by. He couldn't make out any street signs until they had gone a few blocks. Then he saw a green sign that said Halsted.

Close to Lake Michigan two huge apartment buildings rose on either side of the road. They were in Lincoln Park, and a few minutes later the men found a marina and parked the van by the pier.

"Too many people around," the driver said. "It'll thin out in a few minutes."

Ryan shook as he prayed.

Judd had never seen Chaya this excited. Loretta was busy on the phone. Vicki had joined Judd and Chaya in Bruce's office.

"You're not going to believe this," Chaya said. "I typed our names into the computer and hit the Search key. You guys show up all the way through here."

"I thought this was just his sermon notes," Vicki said.

"No," Chaya said. "He included lots of personal impressions of his friends. I think we have the answer to a question about Ryan."

Chaya typed in Ryan's name, and Judd read over her shoulder.

"Ryan has finally made his decision," Bruce

had written, *"and we are all very thankful. He is the last of the four to see the truth and trust Christ for forgiveness of sins. I pray God will use him mightily in the time we have left."*

"I remember that day," Vicki said.

"The interesting stuff comes a couple hundred pages later," Chaya said as she clicked the keyboard. "Read this."

"Ryan's idea has put me in a difficult situation," Judd read. *"If I trust him with this information, it could jeopardize my relationship with the adult Tribulation Force."*

"What's he talking about?" Vicki said.

"I haven't been able to figure it out," Chaya said. "But it's clear from the other stuff Bruce said that it has something to do with the Bibles Ryan was collecting. Another section of the file mentioned an underground shelter."

"I remember Bruce saying something about how we need to prepare for the worst," Vicki said, "but where would the shelter be?"

"Remember the excavation they did a few months ago?" Judd said.

"Yeah, sure, but that was just a construction project, wasn't it?" Vicki said.

"Maybe not," Judd said.

The next entry by Bruce read, *"I've decided to go with Ryan's idea and still keep the integrity of the project downstairs. Hopefully, this will*

*provide Ryan with the space and secrecy he
needs, without compromising the project."*

"I don't get it," Vicki said. "Is he talking
about the downstairs of his house?"

"I don't think so," Judd said. "Follow me."

Ryan mumbled through the tape over his
mouth.

"Save your breath," the short man said,
"we're not givin' you a chance to scream for
help."

Ryan cocked his head and rolled his eyes.

"I think he wants to tell us something," the
driver said. He climbed in the back, pulled
out a gun, and waved it at Ryan. "If you open
your yap and yell, you won't do it twice,
understand?"

Ryan nodded, and the man jerked the tape
from his mouth.

"I'm trying to figure this out," Ryan gasped
through the pain.

"He doesn't need to figure anything out,"
the short man said. "Put the tape back on."

"I'm not gonna cry for help," Ryan said.
"But before you guys whack me, I gotta know
why you'd throw away such a golden opportunity."

The driver squinted.

Ryan continued. "I mean, I can understand
why you'd grab a girl like Darrion. Her dad's

loaded. But what I don't understand is why you'd let me go without even trying to get in touch with my family."

"Are you saying your family can offer us something for your safe return?" the driver said. "As in, money?"

"He's bluffin'," the short man said.

Ryan shook his head. "It just doesn't make good business sense. I mean, I heard you guys talking about how you were going to split the money you got from Darrion." Ryan laughed. "You guys need to start thinking bigger."

The short man grabbed the tape and was about to put it back over Ryan's mouth when the driver grabbed his arm. "Let the kid talk," he said. "What have we got to lose?"

"From what I gather," Ryan said, "you guys aren't working with Darrion's parents. That's your first mistake. You have no control."

"They're payin' us okay for the risk we're takin'," the short man said.

"Are they?" Ryan said. "Compared with what Mr. Stahley is able to pay, I don't think so."

"Our boss isn't in it for the money," the short man said. "He wants the Stahley guy to—"

"Shut up!" the driver said. "Don't tell him everything you know."

"All I'm saying is you've got a bird in your hand that will pay a limited amount," Ryan said. "But you're throwing away the goose that laid the golden egg."

"And you're the goose?" the driver said.

Ryan nodded.

The short man laughed and slapped the tape back on Ryan's mouth. "Let's get it over with," he said.

"And what if he's telling the truth?" the driver said. "What if we are sellin' ourselves short?"

"I can see it in his eyes," the short man said. "Drive to the end of the pier and we'll open the door."

Judd led Chaya and Vicki to the darkened church basement. They walked through the fellowship hall, down a narrow corridor, past the washrooms and the furnace room. They were now at the end of the hallway with no light.

"They did the excavation on the other side of this wall," Judd said. He felt around the concrete blocks. Nothing. They returned to the furnace room, and Judd flipped on

the light switch. A flashlight rested atop
the furnace. Judd flicked it on and scanned
the back wall closely. He found the furnace
and a hot-water heater. Nothing out of the
ordinary.

"Wait," Chaya said as Judd turned to leave.
"That back wall is weird. There's nothing
hanging there or pushed against it. It's
wasted space."

The three felt along the back wall.
Suddenly, Judd found an indentation about
the size of his hand. Judd braced his feet and
pushed hard. The three looked in amaze-
ment as a section of the wall slid open.

"I'm not goin' in there," Vicki said.

"What if Ryan's down here, hiding?" Judd
said. "What if he's hurt?"

"We know that can't be," Vicki said. "Don't
we?"

Vicki followed them in, and Judd pushed
the wall closed behind them. "Whatever's
down here needs to be kept a secret," Judd
said.

There was a smell of wet earth and
cement. The flashlight illuminated a sign
directly in front of them and six steps down:
"Danger! High Voltage. Authorized Person-
nel Only."

They moved down the steps and took a

left. Four more steps down was a huge steel door. The sign at the landing of the stairs was duplicated on the door. The knob was locked.

"Dead end," Vicki said.

"Who would have the key?" Chaya said.

"Bruce would," Judd said, "but it doesn't have a keyhole. There must be some other way to get it open." He jiggled the door and banged on it. No luck. Judd led them back up the steps to the entrance.

"Wait," Vicki said. "Shine the light over here."

Judd pointed the light to the wall behind the secret entrance. They ran their hands over it, and this time Chaya squealed in delight.

"It's a hand print, just like the one outside, only a little lower," Chaya said. She leaned into it, and the wall gave way a few inches. Judd put the flashlight down and helped. They moved inside the darkened room and listened. Vicki felt for a light switch but tripped. Judd heard paper rattling. Then Vicki began to laugh.

"Are you okay?" Judd said as he retrieved the flashlight and shone it in her face.

"This is it!" Vicki said excitedly. "We found it!"

Judd found a light switch.

"Incredible," Chaya said.

Around the room, in stacks of fifty each, were the Bibles Ryan had confiscated. Vicki had knocked over a small stack by the door.

"Look at this," Chaya said.

In the corner was a small table with a lamp. Beside it was a picture of Ryan with his mother and father. Next to it was a picture taken only a few weeks earlier of Ryan and Bruce. He also had photos of Lionel, Vicki, and Judd, a photo of Bruce and his family, and one of Phoenix. In the middle of the table was a spiral notebook. Vicki opened it.

"Bruce said I should keep a diary of the things I think about, so I'm going to do it here," Vicki read out loud. *"Bruce said this could be my secret place. If anything ever happens to me, he can tell the others where I'm hiding the Bibles."*

"There must be hundreds in here," Chaya said.

"We've already given a few hundred away," Judd said. "The room must have been packed."

"Listen to this," Vicki said. *"Sometimes I feel really lonely and I want my mom and dad to come back. I wish they could be here so I could tell them what I've learned and what I know about God. But I do have good friends."* Vicki choked up.

"Maybe we'd better not read it," Judd said.

"I mean, if he's alive and we find him, he'll be mad."

"Yeah," Vicki said. "I like that attitude."

Lionel returned from the police station and sat by the phone, hating every minute. He wanted to do something to find Ryan. But there was nothing he could do. He had called every possible place Ryan could be. As he sat by the phone, he had an overwhelming urge to pray for Ryan, like he was in danger.

"Give him strength, Father God," Lionel prayed. "Watch over him and protect him."

Ryan felt the crisp lake air on his face as the men drove toward the water. He could hear the sound of cars on nearby Lake Shore Drive, but no people were in sight. Even if he did manage to scream, nobody would hear him.

"Open the door and toss him," the driver said.

Ryan looked at the murky water. If it was shallow, he could get his legs under him. He might be able to bob long enough to stay alive. But if the water was more than six feet deep, there was no hope.

The short man dragged him to the edge of

the van. Ryan saw the movement of the water as it lapped against wooden posts. *Too deep,* he thought.

"I'll count to three," the driver said. The short man rocked Ryan back and forth as he counted. "One . . . two . . ."

On the third time, the man stopped and stripped the tape from Ryan's mouth. "You get one more chance. Tell us about your old man."

Ryan trembled, half from fear and half from the cold. "I-I told you," he stammered, "he puts Darrion's father to shame."

"How much is he worth?" the driver said.

"He owns a lot of cows," Ryan said. "Like, on a thousand hills."

"So he's a rancher?" the short man said.

"Sort of," Ryan said. "My father is rich. He has a mansion, and there's a room he's preparing for me right now."

"What's his name?" the driver said. "We ever heard of him?"

"You've probably seen some of the things he's made," Ryan said, "but I don't know that you know him."

"And you think he'll pay?" the driver said.

"He's already paid a lot for me," Ryan said. "I was adopted into his family. It cost an awful lot."

"Adopted?" the short man said.

"Yeah, I met his son, and he introduced me to his father. After that, they made me part of the family."

The two looked at each other. "Sounds hard to believe," the driver said. "Rich guy takes a kid in and makes him an heir?"

The short man shrugged. "How can we reach your dad?" he said.

"I'm not telling until we get back to the house," Ryan said.

"What?!" the driver said.

"If I give you the number, you can throw me in the lake, then call to get the ransom."

"We could just throw you in now and be done with the whole thing," the short man said, tipping Ryan on his side.

"True," Ryan said. "And then you'd probably miss the biggest payday of your life. What my dad can give you could last you forever."

"I got my doubts that anybody would want a kid like this back," the driver said. "But I guess it's worth a try."

Ryan watched the street signs carefully on the way back. If he could somehow get away, he wanted to know where to run. Ryan gave them Judd's number.

"Who do we ask for?" the short man said.

"Ask for Ryan Daley's father," Ryan said. Ryan prayed someone would be home and would say the right thing to keep him alive. *At least I've been outside and know what I'm up against*, Ryan thought.

Darrion was surprised to see him. It looked like she had been crying. Ryan put his finger to his lips.

"Look," the driver said, "we get in touch with the kid's dad. If it's a hoax, we whack the kid."

"But if he's telling the truth," the short man said, "he knows where we are and what we look like."

"Do I look stupid?" the driver said. "If the dad's rich, we tell him the kid's okay, set up a drop site, and whack him anyway. The kid's outta the picture, and we're a million or two richer."

"What about the boss?" the short man said.

"The boss never knows the difference."

The two were silent a moment. "I'd only change one thing," the short man said. "When you call the guy, make it five million."

FIVE

The Call

LIONEL answered the phone on the first ring. The caller ID didn't display the number.

"I'm looking for Ryan Daley's father," a strange voice said.

"Excuse me?" Lionel said. *Ryan's dad is dead,* Lionel thought.

"Ryan Daley's father," the man said. "Do you know where he is?"

Lionel bit his cheek. This could be the break they were looking for. "Yeah, he's not here," Lionel said. "Can I take a message?"

"No," the man said. "When will he be back?"

"I can't say," Lionel said.

The line clicked. Lionel called Judd. "I think we have our first really good clue," Lionel said.

"I thought you were a goner," Darrion said. "I was thinking about all the nice things I'd say at your funeral."

"You don't know how close I came," Ryan said. He explained what had happened and the clues he had learned. Darrion shook her head.

"I haven't told you everything," she said. "You know how I said my aunt and uncle disappeared? Well, they did, but the whole thing was suspicious. My dad started checking it out."

"Wait," Ryan said. "You never really said what your father did for a living."

"He does security stuff. You know, making sure the big guys are safe. He helps out with some of the military jobs, too."

"Military jobs?" Ryan said.

"Disposing of the nuclear weapons," she said. "Planning military assaults, that kind of thing."

Ryan raised his eyebrows. "No wonder your dad's rich," he said. "They have to trust you big time to put you in that position."

"That's just it," she said. "When he started looking into what happened to my aunt and uncle, he got the feeling that somebody didn't like it very much. But he didn't stop."

"Did he find out what happened?"

"He never told me a lot about it directly. I'd pick up things here and there when he talked with my mom. It seemed like the more he looked, the more convinced he became that there was something to the story my aunt and uncle were telling. You know, the Bible and everything. It seemed like what they believed got them killed."

"So they didn't disappear?" Ryan said.

"They were being held in custody in Romania. This was back before there was a Global Community. They had said something against Nicolae Carpathia. I don't know what. My dad found the place where they were held. They weren't released, they just disappeared."

I know what happened to them, Ryan thought.

Lionel talked again with Mrs. Fogarty. She said she would do what she could. When Judd came in, Lionel told him more about the conversation with the mysterious caller.

"Could it have been somebody from a hospital or the police?" Judd said.

"Don't think so," Lionel said. "Whoever it was sounded like they were outside. Either a cell phone or a pay phone."

Judd called the phone company but was told incoming calls could not be traced. "But this is a serious matter," Judd said. "If the police ask you to trace it, can you?"

"Only in extreme cases," the operator said.

Lionel sat down and scribbled some notes on a pad of paper. "This is what we know. We have Ryan's mangled bike and an old lady who says she saw him being taken from the street."

"In a white van," Judd said.

"We know Ryan would have called us. And he's not in any of the hospitals or morgues in the area."

"At least as far as we can tell," Judd said.

"We know Ryan isn't in his Bible hideout," Lionel said. "And now we can add this strange guy who asks for Ryan's dad."

"If it was from a hospital or the police, the guy would have asked for a parent," Judd said.

"And he would have identified himself as an official," Lionel said.

"Next time he calls, we'll let him speak with Ryan's dad," Judd said.

Ryan told Darrion his story. He began with his friend Raymie and his mom. She was just like Darrion's aunt and uncle. Always going to church. Always talking about God. Raymie lived differently and didn't do some of the stuff Ryan did. Ryan couldn't understand it.

Then, when Raymie and his mom disappeared with the rest, Ryan found a group of kids and a pastor who explained what had happened. Jesus Christ had returned for those who truly believed in him. It was the only explanation that made any sense.

"That sounds so weird," Darrion said.

"It did to me, too, when I first heard it," Ryan said. "But think about it. People vanish. Nothing but their clothes left behind. Babies disappear. Unborn children too. How can you explain that?"

"What about the pastor you met? Why wasn't he taken?"

Ryan explained Bruce Barnes's story in detail. Just talking about Bruce made Ryan ache to see him again. "It sounds like your dad was thinking a lot about spiritual stuff when he looked into the deaths of your aunt and uncle," Ryan said.

"I think you're right," Darrion said. "In the last few weeks he and Mom have been up late talking. They even started reading the Bible, if you can believe that."

"I can," Ryan said. "I never read the Bible before, but now that I have people who can help me understand it, I—"

The door flew open, and the short man yelled, "Get over here, kid!"

"Did you get in touch with my dad?" Ryan said.

The man jerked Ryan into the next room.

"I talked to some kid who said he didn't know when your dad would be back."

"That was probably Lionel," Ryan said. "He's my brother."

"My partner and I have a bad feeling about this. If we don't get a response soon, we're gonna cut you loose."

Ryan didn't want to think about what that phrase meant.

"My father's a busy guy, but I know he really cares for me. Why don't you give him a number to call you back?"

"What do you think, we're stupid?" the short man said. "But if we don't get in touch with him on the next call, that's it."

Vicki met with Chloe at the church. She told Chloe the latest about Ryan. Chloe was visibly upset by the news. "So much has happened so quickly," she said. "We were on our way to see Bruce when the bombings started. Then, after my dad discovered Bruce's body, Nicolae Carpathia called him. They flew my dad and Amanda away in a chopper."

"Do you know where they went?" Vicki said.

"We believe they're with Carpathia, but we don't know where," Chloe said. "When O'Hare was bombed, I was afraid they might have been caught in the middle, but we're assuming they're safe."

Lionel and Judd came in.

"Who's at the house?" Vicki said.

"We forwarded the calls to Judd's cell phone," Lionel said.

"Any luck on Sergeant Fogarty and the trace?" Vicki said.

"None," Lionel said. "Is Mr. Williams here?"

Chloe led them to Buck, who was waiting for Donny Moore, a computer specialist who attended the church. Buck said he'd be glad to pose as Ryan's father. He and Chloe needed to leave soon, but they would do everything they could.

Chaya rushed into the office with a stack of papers, and Chloe excused herself to talk with Buck.

"I've been going through more of Bruce's manuscript," Chaya said. "Bruce's read on Revelation convinced him that we were at the end of the eighteen-month period of peace, which came right after the treaty Israel made with the Antichrist."

"He's been right about everything so far," Judd said.

"Hang on," Chaya said. "Bruce thinks what's next is worse."

Chaya handed them a photocopy of a few pages of Bruce's notes.

"If I am right, and we can set the beginning of the Tribulation at the time of the signing of the treaty and what was then known as the United Nations," Bruce had written, *"we are perilously close to and must prepare for the next prediction in the Tribulation timeline. The Red Horse of the Apocalypse."*

Lionel smiled. "Remember when Ryan first heard about these verses?" he said. "He told me later he'd started to hate horses."

Vicki put a hand on Lionel's shoulder.

"Look at Revelation, chapter six," Chaya said. Each member grabbed a Bible and read verses three and four: "When the Lamb broke the second seal, I heard the second living being say, 'Come!' And another horse appeared, a red one. Its rider was given a mighty sword and the authority to remove peace from the earth. And there was war and slaughter everywhere."

"This will affect all people," Chaya said. "Bruce believed these verses refer to a prediction of global war."

"Isn't that what we're in now?" Lionel said.

"Let me come back to that," Chaya said. "Bruce thought this would likely be known as World War III. It will be started by the

Antichrist, and yet he will rise as the great solver of it, a real peacemaker."

"Carpathia, the great liar," Vicki said.

"He will use this opportunity to gain more power for himself," Chaya said. "After that, Bruce believed the next two horses would be loosed—the black horse of plague and famine and the pale horse of death. I've been doing more study, and I think what we've seen so far is just the start of the war. The strike on the Nike base and the hospital was isolated."

"Tell that to New York City," Judd said.

"But even there," Chaya said, "the bombings seemed targeted. And we don't know how much is coming from the militia and how much from the Global Community."

"I could see Nicolae bombing a place and blaming it on someone else," Vicki said.

Judd's phone rang. He handed the phone to Lionel and quickly went out of the room.

Darrion seemed interested in Ryan's story, but cautious. As they talked, he bent one of his soda cans in half, then worked it until it broke in two. He took the razor-sharp edge and began scratching at one of the small panes of glass in the corner of the window.

"What are you doing?" Darrion said.

"If I'm right," Ryan said, "I may not have that much time before the guys discover the truth about my father."

"You told me your father was dead," Darrion said. "I thought one of the rules you lived by was that you weren't supposed to lie."

"I didn't lie to them," Ryan said. "My father does own a lot of cattle and land, and he is making a place for me."

"I don't get it."

Ryan stopped and turned toward her. "God is my father. There's a verse in the Bible that says he owns the cattle on a thousand hills. And Jesus said he was going to prepare a place for people who believed in him. All of that's true."

"But you knew those guys would think you were talking about your real dad."

"I didn't plan it that way," Ryan said. "It was the first thing that popped into my head. My family now is everyone who believes in Christ. One day, we'll all be together."

"How can you be so sure about it?" Darrion said. "That's what always got me about my aunt and uncle. They acted like they knew. I'd love to be sure of myself, but I don't want to throw away my brain."

"It's not about being sure of yourself," Ryan said. He dusted the scrapings from the window ledge and put the can down. "That's the difference between what Enigma Babylon One World Faith teaches and what I believe. The new religion says you should trust yourself. Decide for yourself which way you should go. As long as you follow your inner voice, you'll be okay."

"That's not exactly what they teach, but go on."

"The new religion says I should put my faith in faith, in whatever I find that makes me feel like I'm following God."

"You've got a problem with that?" Darrion said.

"Yeah," Ryan said, "it's just plain wrong. You can't let your feelings guide what you believe. You believe what's true."

"And what *is* true? One person's truth might not fit somebody else. See, now *you're* being exclusive."

"You shouldn't believe in belief," Ryan said. "You believe in God. In a person. That's what's true." Ryan could tell he was losing her. "Look, you can't see what's outside now, but if we can get this windowpane out, we can communicate with somebody on the outside."

"So?"

"You're trusting me because I've been

outside. For all you know, we might be in some cornfield with nobody around, but you trust me because I've seen it."

"I still don't know what that has to do with—"

"God showed himself to us through Jesus," Ryan said. "He sent his only Son so we could know what God is like. He was God. And he not only showed us the truth, but he also took the punishment for the bad things we've done."

"I believe Jesus was a good person and all," Darrion said, "but I still don't see how you can be so sure."

"I'm not sure because I have great faith. I'm sure because God is great. God showed how great he was by the miracles he performed. The Bible predicts the disappearances and the rise of a one-world government. It's coming true all around us."

"Now you're really talking like my aunt and uncle," Darrion said.

"I don't want to preach to you," Ryan said. "It took me a long time to think it through. But you can't say Jesus was a good man and buy into Enigma Babylon. Jesus said he was the only way to God. And he proved he was God by rising from the dead. That's why I believe in him and can be sure of heaven. It's

true not because I want it to be but because
I'm trusting somebody who's been there."

Darrion squinted and looked at the
window. "Give me the other half of that
can," she said.

"Hello?" Lionel said.

"Yeah, I'm looking for your dad."

"Sure, can I ask who's calling?"

"Tell him it's a friend who knows something about his son."

Judd rushed back in with Buck Williams.
Buck took the phone.

"What can you tell me about Ryan?" Buck
said.

Lionel leaned in close to the phone's
earpiece and heard the man say, "First off, if
you go to the police, you'll never see your
son again. Got that?"

"Is he okay?" Buck said.

"I said, if you go to the po—"

"I got it, all right?" Buck said forcefully.
"Now what about Ryan?"

"Second, if you value the kid's life, you'll
go to the bank and withdraw five million
dollars in cash today."

"I can't get that kind of—"

"Twenties and fifties," the man said.

"I want to talk to him," Buck said. "I want to know he's okay before I do anything."

"Hey, I'm telling you he's okay."

The veins in Buck's neck stood out. "And I'm telling you, either you let me talk with him, or you never see the money."

Buck punched the cell phone and hung up on the man.

"What are you doing?" Lionel said, horrified.

"It's a hunch," Buck said. "I think it'll work. If we can get control of the situation, we might get a clue from Ryan."

"Control?" Lionel said. "You're playing with Ryan's life!"

"Calm down," Buck said. "For some reason, this guy believes Ryan's father is still living and he's rich. If it's money he really wants, he'll do anything to get it."

"And if you're wrong, the guy gets spooked and never calls again," Lionel said. "And we never find out what happened."

"Unlikely," Buck said. "If Ryan really is alive—"

"He's alive!" Lionel said.

"Right," Buck said, "but it won't work if I'm too anxious. Believe me, I've interviewed enough rich people to know how they act. A guy like that would want to know his son was alive before he shelled out the cash."

Buck took the phone and punched a few numbers on the keypad.

"Hello?" Buck said. "Who is this? Where are you, sir? Okay, good." Buck motioned for a pen and paper. "And what's the closest intersection near you?"

Buck scribbled on the page. "All right. Tell me, did you just see a man at that phone? Okay. Thank you." Buck scribbled some more and hung up.

"I dialed the return call," Buck said. "A guy on the street picked it up. The phone is on Michigan Avenue in Chicago."

SIX

Ryan's Clue

JUDD and Lionel stayed with Buck in case the man called again. Donny Moore, a computer whiz, arrived at the church and showed Buck a stack of computer catalogs.

"Whoa," Buck said, "I can see already there are too many choices. Why don't I tell you what I'm looking for, and you tell me if you can deliver?"

"I can tell you right now I can deliver," Donny said. "Last week I sold a guy thirty sub-notebooks with more power than any desktop anywhere. You tell me what you want, I'll get it."

Judd felt a chill go down his spine as Donny said, "When's Bruce gonna be back here?"

"When you said you prayed," Darrion Stahley said, "what did you mean? I know what I do when I meditate, but it sounds like it's something different for you."

Ryan continued working on the window as they talked. "It's like I was saying before, when you pray, you don't follow a bunch of rules or work yourself into a state of mind. You pray to a person."

"I think God's a force in the universe. Why do you say he's a person?"

"A lot of reasons," Ryan said. "The Bible says God created us in his own image. He's communicated with people for thousands of years. And then he showed us exactly what he was like when Jesus—"

The door swung open, and the short man barked for Ryan. Darrion grabbed the soda can from Ryan's hand. "Good luck," she said as he left the room.

Buck asked Donny to sit. "You knew Bruce was sick," Buck said.

"I knew they took him to the hospital, but I just assumed . . ."

Buck touched Donny's arm. "The attack wiped out the hospital," he said. "Bruce didn't make it."

Judd watched as Donny crumpled and fell to his knees. It was painful to go through the feelings again with Donny. "I was able to see him after they recovered his body," Judd said. "Mr. Steele did too, as I understand."

Buck nodded. "I'm really sorry."

Donny looked at him blankly. "Mr. Williams, this has all been hard enough even with Pastor Bruce here. I don't know what we're going to do now."

"Donny," Buck said gravely, "you have an opportunity here to do something for God, and it's the greatest memorial tribute you could ever give to Bruce Barnes."

"Well then, sir, whatever it is, I want to do it."

"First," Buck said, "let me assure you that money is no object."

"I don't want any profit off something that will help the church and God and Bruce's memory."

"Fine. Whatever profit you build in or don't build in is up to you. I just need five of the absolute best, top-of-the-line computers, as small and compact as they can be, but with as much power and memory and speed and communications abilities as you can wire into them."

"You're talking my language, Mr. Williams."

"I hope so, Donny, because I want a computer with virtually no limitations.

I want to be able to take it anywhere, keep it reasonably concealed, store everything I want on it, and most of all, be able to connect with anyone anywhere without the transmission being traced. Is that doable?"

"Well, sir, I can put together something for you like those computers that scientists use in the jungle or in the desert when there's no place to plug in or hook up to."

"Yeah," Buck said. "Some of our reporters use those in remote areas. What do they have, built-in satellite dishes?"

"Believe it or not, it *is* something like that. And I can add another feature for you too."

"What's that?"

"Video conferencing."

"You mean I can see the person I'm talking to while I'm talking to him?"

"Yes, if he has the same technology on his machine."

"I want all of it, Donny. And I want it fast. And I need you to keep this confidential."

"Mr. Williams, these machines could run you more than twenty thousand dollars apiece."

Lionel's eyes were wide. Buck whistled through his teeth.

"Do it," Buck said.

The short man grabbed Ryan by the collar. "Goin' for another ride," he barked. The driver helped tape Ryan's hands together. On their way to the van, Ryan looked for an escape, but none came. The short man stayed close to him. Ryan knew if he did get free, he would probably endanger Darrion's life. He didn't want to do that.

A few people were on the sidewalk when the van drove by. No one looked at them. The men drove downtown and parked across the street from a bank of pay phones.

"Did you talk with my dad?" Ryan said.

"Shut up and listen," the short man said. "This is how it's goin' down. I'm gonna call your old man again and we're gonna let him know his precious little boy is still alive."

"Fine with me," Ryan said.

"But listen to me," the man said, focusing his steely gaze on Ryan. "You say anything other than 'Hello' or 'Hey, Dad, it's me, give them the money,' and we'll go back to the lake for a little swim."

"A long swim." The driver smirked.

"You got it?"

"I got it."

"And if you try to call out for help to anybody when I roll down the window, I'll hang up, and we forget your old man."

"I understand," Ryan said.

The driver pulled into traffic. He made a

U-turn and pulled up to the bank of phones. The short man rolled down his window and dialed the number.

What can I say? Ryan thought. *If I've got only one sentence, or even a few words, what could help Judd and the rest find me?*

Judd was able to reach Sergeant Fogarty and gave him the location of the pay phone the caller had used. Sergeant Fogarty gave Judd his beeper number and a special code. The officer would dispatch someone to the scene if the man called again.

Judd and Lionel helped Buck box the pages from Bruce's printout. Buck told Judd that Chloe was dropping him off at the Chicago bureau office of *Global Community Weekly*.

As Buck and Chloe made their way out to the Range Rover, Buck lugging the heavy carton, he said to Chloe, "If the guy calls back, give him my private number at the office, and you'd better check with The Drake Hotel and be sure our stuff is still there. We'll want to keep that room until we find a place to live out here."

"I was hoping you'd say that," Chloe said. "Loretta is devastated. She's going to need a lot of help. I was thinking we could stay with her."

Buck and Chloe talked about Bruce's funeral. Judd offered the help of the Young Tribulation Force. His cell phone rang. Lionel answered on the second ring as Judd raced to a different phone and quickly dialed Sergeant Fogarty's beeper. If they could keep the man on the phone long enough, there was a chance they could find Ryan.

"Yeah, I'll get him," Lionel said. "Hang on a minute."

Buck held the phone as long as he dared, then said, "I'm here. Do you have Ryan with you?"

Buck gave them the thumbs-up signal.

"Before you let me talk with him, I want to understand your demands," Buck said. "Can any of the four million be in larger bills, like hundreds?"

Buck pulled the phone away from his ear. Judd could hear the man cursing through the earpiece.

Ryan heard the man's tirade. "You know I said five million," he screamed. "Now we're gonna make it six."

The man grabbed Ryan and pulled him to the window of the van.

"Yeah, I like that attitude a lot better," the

man said. "Six it is. Now would you like to hear the sound of your kid's voice?"

The man shoved the mouthpiece into Ryan's face. Ryan froze.

"Talk!" the man yelled.

Ryan opened his mouth, but nothing came out.

"I said talk!" the man said, whacking Ryan in the forehead with the phone.

Ryan gasped and said as clearly as he could, "Darrion Stahley!"

The short man shoved Ryan to the back of the van and threw the phone out the window. Ryan fell toward the door and struggled to stand. He was close to the door handle when the driver floored the accelerator, and Ryan was thrown hard into the rear seat.

"You've done it now, kid," the short man said. "Those are the last words your dad will ever hear you say."

"What did he say again?" Judd said as they went in the church.

"It happened so fast," Buck said. "I know the first word was *Darien,* but I didn't get the second too well. Sounded like he said *stolley.*"

"What in the world could that be?" Lionel said.

"There's a suburb southwest of Chicago

called Darien," Judd said. "Maybe that's where they're holding him."

"Why would they drive all the way downtown to call us?" Lionel said. "And how would they get there so fast?"

"Okay, forget the first word," Judd said. "What's a *stolley*?"

Chaya overheard the conversation and clicked at the church's computer screen. "It sounds more like a name to me," she said, "not a place."

"You think that's the name of the people holding him?" Lionel said.

"I don't know who it is," Chaya said, "but for some reason Ryan chose those words."

Chaya typed in the different possible spellings of the word *stolley*. The Internet search engine provided information about a tennis player, a nineteenth-century geologist, cosmetic surgery centers, and personal pages. On the ninth spelling she slapped the desktop and let out a yell.

"Maxwell Stahley," Chaya said, spelling the name for everyone.

"Who's that?" Lionel said.

"The security magnate," Buck said. "Of course!"

"He's a pretty impressive guy," Chaya said, reading from the screen. "Lives near Chicago.

A member of the Global Community special security force. Owns his own international security business. Looks like he's pretty well off."

"How do you know he's the right one?" Lionel said.

Chaya pointed to the screen. "Married seventeen years to Louise Stahley. One child. A girl. Darrion."

"Bingo," Judd said.

"Weird name," Lionel said.

"You think Ryan is being held by an international agent of the Global Community?" Vicki said.

Darrion screamed when the men threw Ryan into the room. Darrion cut the tape with the edge of the pop can. Ryan huddled close to the door and listened as the two men talked.

"The kid said her name," the short man said.

"So what?" the driver said. "If the guy's ready to shell out six million, the kid can say whatever name he wants."

"You know what happens if the boss finds out?" the short man said, an edge in his voice. "You don't know these people like I do. They won't like us sneaking around behind their backs."

"How are they gonna know?" the driver

said. "The kid says a name. Maybe his dad didn't hear it right or thinks he said something else."

"But if the boss finds out we're doing freelance on the side when we're supposed to be taking care of the girl, we're in trouble."

"Fine," the driver said. "As soon as it gets dark, we take care of the kid. Then we make one more call to the father. Give him a drop site and see what happens."

"And what if the dad doesn't buy it?" the short man said.

"So we're out the cost of the phone call. But if he does buy it, you and me split six million big ones. The boss doesn't have to know."

Ryan crawled close to Darrion and explained what happened.

"Why did you tell them my name?" Darrion said. "Your friends don't know me from Adam. No offense to your religion."

Ryan smiled. "I couldn't think of anything else. I figured if my friends get in touch with your family, they could work together."

Darrion frowned. "I don't know how they'll get in touch with my mom and dad. Our house is like a fortress, and the number's unlisted."

"I have to get out of here before nightfall,"

Ryan said. "How far did you get on that window?"

Darrion pulled back the curtain, and a shaft of light hit Ryan in the face. He ducked his head and saw the sun going down over a water tower in the distance.

"I got this one out while you were gone," she said. "It crashed on the fire escape."

Ryan stuck his head through, but the opening was too small for his shoulders.

"I tried that," she said. "Then I yelled, but the alley's deserted. A couple of cars went by, but they couldn't hear me, I guess."

"Good going," Ryan said. "Now if we can get this bigger pane out, I can climb through and go for help."

"We," Darrion said. "You're not leaving me in here alone."

"Okay," Ryan said. "*We* can climb through and get out of here."

Judd and Vicki looked for the access road to the Stahley mansion. They were only a few miles from Northwest Community Hospital. Chaya had called the headquarters of Maxwell Stahley's business, but she was told he had taken a leave of absence from the company.

"I assume that means he's working for the Global Community and I should lay off,"

Chaya had said. She found an address for the
Stahley home, but it took Judd and Vicki a
half hour to find the hidden road that led
there. Vicki discovered it by poking around
behind a riding stable while Judd asked
directions at a gas station.

The huge estate was triangular and
bordered an exclusive golf course and a forest
preserve. Judd parked in a picnic area, and
the two hiked into the woods.

Twenty minutes later they came to the
twelve-foot iron fence that surrounded the
Stahley property. Judd gave a low whistle
when he saw the house. The lawn was finely
manicured, and several mature trees dotted
the backyard. Judd stood on a stump and
saw a huge pool with a slide in the patio
area.

"See anything?" Vicki said.

"No people," Judd said. "I'm trying to
figure out how we can get over this fence.
There must be some kind of electronic
surveillance system. If this guy is in international security, you'd think—"

Judd stopped and pointed to the sharp
spikes at the top of the fence. A tiny sensor
emitted a thin strand of red light. Judd
scanned the tree line and jogged away, pulling Vicki with him. A hundred yards farther

Judd spotted a tall tree whose limbs stretched across the fence.

"If we can climb out onto that branch, we can drop to the ground on the other side," Judd said. "The limb dips. Looks like it's only about a ten- or fifteen-foot drop."

"Looks higher than that to me," Vicki said, "but I'm game."

Vicki was tentative at first, then she seemed to get the hang of it. When they were past the sensor, Judd grabbed the branch and swung toward the ground.

"It looks even higher when you get up here," Vicki said.

Judd let go and dropped to the ground, tucking his legs underneath him and rolling into a pile of leaves.

"You okay?" Vicki said.

"Fine," Judd said. "Move out on the limb a little farther, it's closer to the ground. I'll help you."

Vicki inched out onto the limb. The branch bent with her weight.

"Swing your legs down and I'll see if I can touch your feet," Judd said.

"I don't need help," Vicki said, losing her grip on the limb and grabbing hard. Judd heard a crack behind her and managed to grab Vicki's feet before the branch gave way and Vicki tumbled to the ground.

"I think the branch hit the sensor," Judd said.

"Thanks a lot for the concern," Vicki said.

Judd put his finger to his lips. He expected some type of alarm. He did hear something—a low rumbling of some sort, but he couldn't place it.

The leaves rustled, and Vicki screamed. In the fading light Judd realized the noise was the pounding of paws on the earth. The growling of dogs. And there was no escape.

With the smaller pane out, Ryan and Darrion set to work on the pane in the middle. It was their best chance of escape.

The door opened, and the driver flashed a light around the room. "Where'd you kids go?" the man said.

Darrion stepped out from behind the curtain. "I have to go to the bathroom again!" she said.

"Then come on," the man said. "We have to leave soon."

Ryan's plan, if the men came for him before he and Darrion were through, was to put the tape loosely over his hands and make a run for it as soon as he was in the garage. But he hoped to use the fire escape. That would give Darrion and him more time to put distance between them and the men before they were missed.

"Don't run," Judd yelled as the dogs neared them. "They'll sense our fear."

"I don't have to run for them to sense my fear," Vicki said.

Judd broke off a stick from the fallen branch and swung it back and forth as the dogs approached. One grabbed the end and hung on as Judd tugged fiercely. The other dogs circled, growling and baring their fangs.

The window was nearly out. A few more chinks in the putty, and Ryan and Darrion would be free. Ryan heard the men outside the door. Darrion quickly put the tape over his wrists, and the two sat on the floor as if they'd been there all afternoon.

"Time to go," the short man said.

SEVEN

Maxwell Stahley

VICKI counted five dogs. One would have been enough to paralyze her with fear. Five were terrifying. Ever since she had been a little girl, dogs like these had given her the creeps. Big and black with huge mouths.

One dog lunged at Judd, and he kicked it in the head, only to have another bite at his pant leg. Judd looked like he was losing his balance, so Vicki took off a shoe and threw it as hard as she could. It hit the dog in the neck. The dog let go momentarily and snapped at her.

"I'm gonna try for the fence—maybe they'll follow me," Judd said. "Go to the house and get help."

"You can't!" Vicki said. "They'll tear you to pieces."

"They'll tear us both to pieces if we stay here," Judd said as he took off. "Run!"

Ryan's heart sank. If they only had a few more minutes they'd be free. But the men were at the door, and they meant business.

Ryan wanted to tell Darrion she needed to accept Christ as her savior before it was too late, but there was no time. He stammered a moment, looked at her, then saw the short man in a mask.

"Wait," Darrion said in a strong voice, "I need to talk with him."

"What's wrong?" he said. "You two love-birds or something?"

Ryan wanted to tackle the man or hit him with the flashlight.

"I need to ask him a few questions," she said.

"You've had plenty of time to talk," the man said as he grabbed Ryan. "Come on, kid."

"You don't understand," Darrion said. "I need to talk with him about his religion."

Ryan furrowed his brow. *Was she serious or just pretending?*

"Religion?" the man said. "You two are back here talkin' about religion?"

"I have to clear a few things up," Darrion said. "Even condemned criminals get a last meal."

The short man shook his head. "No way," he said.

The phone rang in the other room. The short man stiffened, then turned Ryan loose. "Do your talkin'," he said. "I'll be right back."

Ryan took the tape from his hands, and they stepped behind the curtain.

"Is what you said real or just a ploy?" Ryan said.

"Both," Darrion said. "I thought we could talk while we try to get this window out."

"So what did you want to ask?" Ryan said as they furiously scraped at the putty.

"If this God you talk about can do all those miracles, why can't he get us out of here?" she said angrily.

"He can," Ryan said. "He can do anything he wants. Heal the sick. Raise the dead. Sometimes he lets people go through stuff like this."

"Like being killed for no reason?" she said. "It doesn't make sense. Why would a God who's supposed to be good allow a sweet kid like you . . ." Darrion smashed the can against the window. It gave way a fraction of an inch. "It's not fair!"

Ryan touched her shoulder. "I've been trying to think of a way to explain it since we met," he said. "*I've* been wondering why God would put me here. It makes total sense now."

"What are you talking about?" Darrion said.

"Remember the verse I told you about? The one that says God loved us so much that he sent his only Son into the world?"

"Yeah."

"Well, I think God was preparing you and your family all along. He sent your aunt and uncle. Then me. I think he put me here to tell you the truth."

"But they're gonna kill you!" Darrion said.

Ryan smiled. He had the feeling he'd finally solved the riddle. "I promise you, I'm not going without a fight."

"How can you say that?" Darrion said. "Why aren't you scared?"

"I am scared," Ryan said. "But it's clear to me now. God loves you. He cared enough for you that he put me here. Pretty cool, huh?"

"I still don't understand."

"You will," Ryan said. "There's something you need to do, and I don't want to leave before you do it."

Ryan dropped his can.

"We're not gonna get this window out of here, are we?" Darrion said.

"Not before the guy gets back," Ryan said. "But I don't think God let us come all this way for nothing." Ryan grabbed the flashlight.

"You're not going to hit him with that, are you?"

"I'd like to," Ryan whispered, "but I'm thinking of something else."

Ryan bunched the curtain up at the bottom and placed it against the window. "Hold this," he said. "I'm gonna give it a kick. Hopefully the whole pane will come out. When it does, you go through and get down the fire escape as fast as you can. I'll be right behind you."

Ryan gently pushed the door closed and propped two mattresses behind the doorknob. Then he shone the flashlight toward the window. He ran a few steps and jumped into the air feetfirst.

Vicki's heart raced as four of the dogs sprinted toward the fence after Judd. The fifth dog, poised like a loaded gun, stood between her and the house.

Judd was climbing the fence now. When

he was a few feet from the top, the dogs
lunged and bit his pant leg, dragging him
back to the ground.

Vicki knew she had to get help, but the
growling dog before her was inching closer.
She looked into its eyes. Hollow.

"Nice doggie," she said nervously.

The dog lunged at her. Vicki jerked back-
wards. She took off her other shoe and
waved it in front of the dog's face. "Come
and get it," she said, waving it high over her
head.

Vicki threw the shoe as far as she could
and yelled, "Fetch!" Without blinking, the
dog turned and ran.

Vicki was gone, running with bare feet over
the cold ground. She heard Judd struggling
and the dogs at the fence barking. She
couldn't help looking over her shoulder, and
there was the dog, a few yards behind, shak-
ing its head as it tore the shoe to bits.

Vicki hit a sudden slope in the yard, lost
her balance, and fell. When she looked up
the dog was beside her, growling. He
dropped the shoe and inched closer. His
teeth were bared.

"No!" Judd yelled from the fence. "Vicki,
get up!"

But it was too late. There was nothing Vicki

could do but cover her face with her arms and scream.

When Ryan's feet hit the glass, he heard a crunch. The window didn't pop out like he had hoped. He grabbed the curtain and kept his balance. Only half the glass had broken.

"Hey, what's goin' on in there?" the short man said.

Ryan took the flashlight and beat furiously against the window. Shards flew everywhere as the glass shattered and fell through the fire escape.

The short man was at the door now, but he couldn't get in. "Carl, they're breakin' something in there!" he yelled. "And the door's stuck."

The sharp pieces of glass around the window looked like the jagged mouth of a jack-o'-lantern. Ryan ran the flashlight around the window and tried to get it as smooth as possible so they could get through.

Both men lunged at the door. "Why didn't you bring him out in the first place?" the one called Carl shouted.

Ryan helped Darrion through just as the men broke the door open.

"Hurry!" Darrion said.

"Go!" Ryan said, "I'm right behind you."

Ryan went through the opening headfirst, then suddenly stopped. The man had him by his shoe. Ryan kicked with his other foot, but the man wouldn't let go. Someone grabbed his hands and pulled. Darrion.

"Ow!" the man yelped. "I'm cut!"

Ryan landed on Darrion in a heap. They were down the first flight of stairs before the men discovered they couldn't fit through the window. Then Ryan and Darrion were on the ground and running.

"It's not much of a head start," Ryan panted as he caught up with her, "but at least we're free."

The dog was over Vicki, inches from her face, when it perked up its ears. He straightened, whimpered, and ran toward the house. The other four dogs near Judd did the same. They ran past Vicki in a flash, barking and whimpering.

Judd caught up to her. "You okay?" he said.

"Better than your pants," Vicki said. "Why'd the dogs run off like that?"

Judd pointed toward the house. Vicki saw a man standing by a shrub with his arms folded. He had a goatee and was nicely dressed. As they neared, they saw an electronic monitor in his hand. He spoke precisely.

"This is private property," the man said. "You are fortunate the animals didn't hurt you. They are trained to kill."

"Are you Mr. Stahley?" Vicki said.

The man ignored her question. "You came onto my property for a reason. What is it?"

Vicki saw Judd square his jaw. "We're looking for Ryan," he said. "We want him back."

"Ryan who?" the man said. "I know no Ryan."

"Ryan Daley," Judd said. "We talked with him this afternoon. He gave us your daughter's name."

The man looked startled. "Come with me," he said.

Vicki had never seen a home so spotless and so empty. Mr. Stahley led them through a huge, sparkling kitchen. The living room was decorated totally in white. A slender woman with brown hair looked lost on the huge couch.

"Was it them, Max?" the woman said.

Vicki noticed the woman's eyes were red and puffy.

"No, just a couple of kids," Mr. Stahley said.

Vicki and Judd got right to the point.

"We're here because we believe you know where our friend Ryan is," Judd said. "Tell us where he is and we'll leave, no questions asked."

"But we don't even—," Mrs. Stahley said.

Mr. Stahley gave her a look. "Tell me what your friend said," he said to Judd. "You talked with him by phone?"

"To be honest," Judd said, "I don't know if we can trust you. We know you work for the Global Community."

Mr. Stahley raised a hand. "Let me tell you our circumstances. Our daughter, Darrion, was taken from us this morning. She was at the riding stables where she goes every day. We received a call from her captors that she is well. That is all we know."

"I'm sorry for you," Vicki said.

"Now tell us about your friend," Mr. Stahley said.

Judd told them. When he was finished, Mr. Stahley scratched his chin.

"Is Ryan your brother?" Mrs. Stahley said.

"In a sense," Vicki said. She quickly explained that they had found each other after the disappearances. When she mentioned that a pastor had actually helped unite them, Judd flinched. Vicki noticed a change in the Stahleys as well.

"How much are they asking?" Judd said.

"Darrion's captors do not want money. They have taken her because of my position with the Global Community."

"You mean they're with the militia?" Judd said.

"No. It comes from within the Global Community. Let us say I have been somewhat at odds with the leadership regarding the current engagement."

"I don't understand," Vicki said. "Why would people from the Global Community want to kidnap your daughter?"

Mr. Stahley explained the situation with his brother and sister-in-law. "After I took this position with the Global Community, I began to look into the circumstances more fully. The further I looked, the more I was told I should not look."

"They were being held by the Global Community for being Christians?" Vicki said.

"They were being held by Nicolae Carpathia," Mr. Stahley said, "before the world knew him. My brother and his wife were working with the church in Romania. They were outspoken Christians."

"I still don't understand why Darrion was kidnapped," Vicki said.

"A few days ago I objected to the targets

the potentate himself suggested," Mr. Stahley said. "After that they cut me off."

"Targets?" Judd said.

"The bombings here and around the world have been planned," Mr. Stahley said gravely. "The loss of innocent lives disturbs me greatly. I threatened to go to the media. That is when Darrion was taken from us."

"And you think if you keep quiet, she'll be returned," Judd said.

"We have to think that!" Mrs. Stahley said. "We have no indication of where she is. I have tapped every source I know. Have you any idea where Ryan is?"

"Chicago," Judd said. "The ransom calls came from the North Side."

"Why would Ryan be mixed up in all this?" Vicki said.

"Perhaps your friend somehow got in the way of Darrion's captors."

Vicki felt frustrated. All the talk of the inner workings of the Global Community made her even madder at Nicolae Carpathia. She wanted to find Ryan and bring him home. She wanted everything to be okay again, but it wasn't. And it didn't look like things would ever be okay again as long as Nicolae was in control.

"What do we do now," Vicki said, "sit and wait?"

"There is nothing I can do," Mr. Stahley said. "I am under constant observation. No doubt you were detected when you came over the fence."

The phone rang. Mr. Stahley spoke in hushed tones. When he returned he was ashen faced. "Darrion remains unharmed," he said. "Within the hour cities around the world will be annihilated."

"What does *annihilated* mean?" Vicki asked.

Mr. Stahley's voice was grave. "*Annihilated* means just what it sounds like it means— totally destroyed."

"What cities?" Judd said.

"Nicolae Carpathia said that he intends to make North America an object lesson to those who oppose the Global Community. Attacks will hit Montreal, Toronto, Dallas, Mexico City, Washington, D.C., New York, Los Angeles, San Francisco. . . ." Mr. Stahley's voice trailed off.

"What?" Mrs. Stahley said.

"And Chicago . . ."

Though she was smaller, Darrion was able to keep up with Ryan well. They came to a cross street. Ryan tried to stop a passing car, but the driver honked his horn and drove past.

They both screamed as they ran, but the noise of the nearby L track drowned them out.

Ryan ran to an apartment building. He made it through the outer door, but the inner one was controlled by a buzzer. He gave up and ran back outside. He heard a garage door opening and doors slamming.

"This way!" Darrion said, as she ran for the abandoned building.

Ryan could only make out the word *candy* on the rickety sign in front. Windows were broken from the second floor to the top. The rest of the building was boarded with plywood. Darrion raced ahead of Ryan to the back. Burned-out trash cans lined the wall. The men Ryan had seen earlier were gone.

"Stop here," Ryan said. He peeked around the corner and saw the van. When it passed, they both jumped behind a trash can. The van slowed, then sped up and zoomed to the end of the street. Trash littered the parking lot, and weeds grew through the broken asphalt.

"Not many places to hide," Darrion said, looking at the emptiness behind them. They could see the Chicago skyline to the south. "Who would have thought you could be in a city this big and feel so alone."

"If we can make it to a phone, we'll be in

good shape," Ryan said. "A gas station or a restaurant or something."

Gravel spun behind them. Ryan turned as the van raced across the empty lot toward them.

"We have to get inside," Ryan said. "They'll catch us for sure out in the open."

They sprinted to the front and pulled at the boards until one gave way. They climbed through the small opening just as the van rounded the corner. Ryan turned on the flashlight, and the carpet seemed to move. Then he realized it wasn't carpeting. Rats.

"I want to get outta here!" Darrion said.

"Keep moving," Ryan said.

They climbed over the rats and out the door of the musty office. Around the corner was the factory area. A heavy layer of dust covered the machinery. The place smelled like the inside of an old refrigerator. They found a stairwell and ran up a few floors. More offices. A lunchroom. More rats.

"What are we gonna do now?" Darrion whispered.

"We have to hide," Ryan said. "If those guys catch me, I'm finished."

"How about if I let them catch me and I tell them you ran for help," Darrion said.

"I couldn't ask you to do that," Ryan said.

"Besides, they'd probably move you and there'd be no way to find you."

Ryan chose the fourth floor. They ran to the other end and found a phone on an old desk. Ryan picked it up, but there was no dial tone.

"Look at this," Darrion said. She pointed to a hole in the wall and an empty space inside. "It looks like a safe was in here. If we could get inside and move something in front of the opening, they'd never find us."

They heard the men ripping boards from the side of the house.

"Hurry!" Ryan said.

Darrion swept their tracks from the dust. Then they ran around the fourth floor, into and out of rooms.

When they heard the sound of the men on the stairs they retreated to their hiding place and pulled the desk tight against the wall. The safe hadn't been huge, but the space was big enough for Ryan and Darrion to sit cross-legged and listen.

"They've definitely been up here," the short man said when the two men walked near them. The man's cell phone rang. The one named Carl answered. "Yes, sir," he said, "everything's fine."

Ryan punched Darrion in the shoulder. "Right," he whispered.

"We'll move her first thing in the morning, boss," Carl said. "What time you want us there? Okay. No problem. We'll call you from there."

"What'd he say?" the short man said.

"He said he'd meet us at sector four tomorrow morning," Carl said.

"Great," the short man said. "Now all we gotta do is find the little vermin."

EIGHT

The Chase

JUDD and Vicki jumped into Mr. Stahley's silver Mercedes and watched the man maneuver the car swiftly through the security gauntlet. Mrs. Stahley had supplied Vicki with new socks and a pair of shoes.

"I don't care who's watching," the man said, "I'm going to save my daughter."

They sped toward the expressway that led to Chicago. Mr. Stahley zigzagged through slower traffic, rode on the shoulder, and screeched around construction cones.

Judd gave Mr. Stahley the location of the pay phone. Mr. Stahley punched up the cross streets on his in-dash computer, and the screen flashed the correct route.

"I think we have company back here," Vicki said.

Judd turned to see a late-model car following the Mercedes.

"I see them," Mr. Stahley said. "They've been with us since we left the house."

"If they were any closer," Vicki said, "they'd be in front of us."

"Global Community," Mr. Stahley said. "They know I'm out of my safety zone. But if they dispose of me, Darrion might be safe."

"You can't bank on that," Judd said. "We have to find her before the bombing starts."

"Hang on," Mr. Stahley said as he pushed the accelerator to the floor.

The men came close to the desk, then clomped down the hall.

"They were so warm, and now they're getting colder and colder," Darrion said.

"When they move to the next floor," Ryan said, "we have to do something. The way I see it, we can hunker down here and hope they leave, or we can kick our offense into gear."

"I have a feeling you think we should do the latter."

"Exactly," Ryan said. He explained his plan. Darrion was skeptical at first, bringing up objection after objection. Then she said, "If it weren't for you, I'd still be in that dingy apartment. I'll do whatever you say."

They quietly moved the desk and stole into the hallway. The men were above them now. Darrion and Ryan timed their actions to the movements of the men. When they heard noise, they moved. When they didn't, they stopped.

Ryan led the way to the lunch area and put his plan in motion.

Judd watched as the car behind them followed closely. Once, Mr. Stahley cut from the extreme left lane to an exit on the right. The car behind them nearly crashed into a truck. The truck swerved, narrowly missing the car, and careened into a wall. Then the Global Community guards were again behind them.

"How important is it for us to lose these guys?" Judd said.

"If we want to find Darrion and your friend," Mr. Stahley said, "we have to lose them. It's their job to keep us away, but—"

"If that's true," Vicki interrupted, "why don't we let those guys lead us to Darrion and Ryan?"

"What do you mean?" Judd said.

"If they're trying to keep us away, they must know where the kids are being held. If we can somehow lose them and make them think we know where we're going, they'd go right to the hideout, wouldn't they?"

"Brilliant," Mr. Stahley said.

"Yeah," Judd said, "but how are we gonna lose them and follow them at the same time?"

"Brace yourself," Mr. Stahley said as he pulled onto the shoulder and slammed on his brakes. Judd heard the squeal of tires and then a sickening crunch as the car behind them smashed into them.

Mr. Stahley opened the glove box and handed Judd two small items. "Stick this one on their front tire, and put this somewhere under the car, out of sight," he said. "It's magnetized."

Mr. Stahley got out of the car and calmly walked back. Judd slipped his cell phone to Vicki and slithered out of the car. He crawled on the ground, praying he wouldn't be seen.

"Do it now," Ryan whispered.

Darrion was inside the entrance to the fourth-floor lunchroom facing the stairs. "Here goes," she said softly, then with a loud voice shouted, "Hey, Carl, get yourself down here!"

Ryan crouched behind the door to the stairwell and watched as Carl came running. The short man was farther away. When Carl got to the bottom of the stairs, Darrion was in clear view.

"I got you now!" the man said gleefully.

I think not, Ryan thought.

Carl's feet flew out from under him as he hit the slick mixture of leftover candy goo that Ryan had put together. The man slid from the door to Darrion's feet.

"I'll be needing this," she said politely, and before the man could protest, she grabbed his cell phone and ran toward the back of the room.

"Got it!" she yelled triumphantly.

Carl tried to get up, but his hands and feet were so slick he flopped like a walrus. When the short man rushed into the room, Carl called out, but it was too late. The short man went down in a heap and slid into Carl, who was on all fours. When he hit, they both went face first into the slime.

Ryan turned and hit the stairwell two and three steps at a time. He raced to the front of the building. Darrion had taken the back stairs and was there a few seconds later.

Ryan grabbed the cell phone and punched the familiar numbers as he ran.

"What's happening?" Vicki said as the Mercedes sped away.

"Not to worry," Mr. Stahley said. The car was right behind them again. Mr. Stahley gave a nod, and Judd pushed a button on a small black box. Immediately the car behind them skidded to the right and stopped. Vicki saw the two men exit the car and shake their fists in the air.

"I don't understand," Vicki said.

"Judd placed a transmitter on their car. I'll be able to follow it here on the screen."

"But how are we supposed to follow them if they're on the side of the road?"

"Judd also placed a small explosive device on the front right tire," Mr. Stahley said. "By the time they change the tire and get back on the road, we'll be a safe distance away and can follow them."

Vicki was amazed. "You have those things just lying around?" she said.

"I keep a few odds and ends for emergencies," Mr. Stahley said as he looked in the rearview mirror. It was the first time Vicki had seen him smile.

"They could have killed you," Vicki said.

"I think I surprised them. I walked to the back of their car to give Judd enough time. It was a calculated risk, but it worked."

Judd's cell phone rang. Vicki answered, and it was Lionel.

"You have to tell me what's going on," Lionel said.

The home phone was busy. Ryan called the church but got the answering machine. Mr. Williams's voice was on it. He didn't listen to the message.

Ryan and Darrion ran through the garbage-strewn lot behind the factory and up over a mound of dirt. The elevated train tracks snaked through the neighborhood. Ryan could make out a stop about three blocks away. If nothing else, they could get lost in the crowd. As they ran, Ryan dialed Judd's cell phone number. Busy.

Great, he thought, *I finally get to a phone and I can't talk to anybody!* He punched the numbers for Bruce's house, but before he could push the Send button, the cell phone rang.

Ryan stopped. Darrion looked over her shoulder. "Answer it," she said.

"Hello?"

"Who is this?" a man said.

"I've got the same question," Ryan said. "Who are you?"

"Where's Carl?"

"That's a lot of questions. How about an answer from you?" Ryan said.

"Put Carl on the line now!" the man said.

"Well, he's in kind of a sticky situation. I don't think he'd want me to use up his cell minutes. Better go."

Ryan hung up and immediately dialed Judd's number again. Still busy.

"This way," Darrion yelled, and she led Ryan underneath the L tracks. A train approached above them with a deafening clatter. In the dimming light, sparks flew from the rail overhead. Abandoned cars and shopping carts littered their path. They hit a cross street. A police car rounded the corner, its lights flashing. Darrion and Ryan waved their arms wildly, but the car sped on, ignoring their cries for help.

"Dial 9-1-1!" Darrion shouted.

"Duh," Ryan said. "Why didn't *I* think of that?"

The line rang and rang. Then Ryan heard a recording.

"Due to the heavy number of calls—," the voice said.

Ryan punched the phone off and tried Judd's phone again. Still busy.

They were close now. People stood in line up ahead. The two sprinted into the street and headed for the entrance to the L stop. From their left the white van shot in front of them. The short man jumped out.

"Thought you could get away, huh?" the man said.

"Lionel's going crazy at home," Vicki said.

"I hope we have something good to report next time we talk," Judd said. "Let me have the phone."

The short man grabbed Darrion. He was still covered with goo. She bit the man's arm and kicked his legs. Carl jumped out of the van and ran to help. But Ryan was there.

"Hey, Candyman," Ryan yelled. "There's some guy on the phone for you. Wants to know where Darrion is. Wanna talk to him?"

Ryan threw the phone in the air, and the short man watched as it smacked against the underside of the train tracks. In that split second Darrion kicked him hard and slipped free. The short man doubled over in pain. Carl tried to grab her, but she darted behind the van and into the street. A car screeched to a halt. Someone screamed.

Ryan grabbed the phone, dodged both men, and rushed around the van. A man was standing in the middle of the street with his car door open.

"She ran right out in front of me!" the man said.

Ryan prepared for the worst. He looked at the pavement in front of the car. No body.

"Where is she?" Carl yelled.

The man in the car held his hand over his chest like he was in pain. "She ran right out," he said again. Then Ryan saw Darrion's boots as she bolted up the stairs. The cashier was yelling at her. The next second the cashier yelled at Ryan as he vaulted over the turnstile.

"Call the police!" Ryan shouted to the lady behind the glass.

Judd's cell phone rang.

"Judd," a familiar voice said, "it's Ryan."

Judd nearly broke down from relief. "Ryan!" he shouted.

"Look, I can't explain right now, but I need help."

"Tell me where you are," Judd said.

The train pulled into the station as Ryan and Darrion rushed onto the platform. The men were coming up the steps. The train doors opened and people streamed out. As Ryan and Darrion ran for the front car, Ryan heard a droning sound above him. He glanced up in time to see a plane streak by. It looked like the same type of plane he had seen earlier in the day in Mt. Prospect.

"We're at the L," Ryan said to Judd. "I don't know which stop. The train just got here."

"Is Darrion with you?" Judd said.

"You figured it out?" Ryan said. "She's right here. We just made it onto the L, but the guys are getting close."

"Ryan, we're in Chicago. Tell us where to go. Which L line are you on?"

"I don't know," Ryan said.

"Ask somebody!" Judd screamed.

Ryan and Darrion hunkered down behind a seat and watched the men push their way onto the platform. The cascade of people had slowed them. Ryan looked up to see the train doors closing.

The conductor spoke over the scratchy speakers. "This is Ravenswood, the Brown Line. Next stop, Diversey. Next stop, Diversey. Stand clear of the doors."

When Ryan glanced back, he couldn't see the men.

"Did they get on?" Darrion said.

Ryan shrugged and told Judd their next stop as the train pulled out. A few moments later someone in the front screamed, "Look out!"

A plane swept low above the buildings, and Ryan saw the explosion. The train rocked, and the cell phone went dead. In the mayhem Ryan turned and saw the two men looking through the window of the next car. Ryan looked to the front and saw a fireball in front of the train. The tracks had been blown to bits and they were heading right for the chasm.

Ryan and Darrion grabbed a metal pole and braced themselves. The train stopped before the gaping hole. Everyone breathed a sigh of relief. Some clapped.

"That was close," Darrion said.

"Yeah, but it looks like we have company," Ryan said, pointing toward the door.

People around them were crying. Some were banging on the doors to get outside.

"I need to tell you something," Darrion said. "I've made my decision."

Ryan sat up straight. "What do you mean?"

"You know," she said, "about God and everything. What you said makes a lot of sense. I think he did send you to tell me the truth. I'm ready."

Ryan's eyes widened and he smiled.

Before he could say another word, another explosion pummeled the tracks. It felt like an earthquake. The train tipped and Ryan saw the ground. If the train fell that way, the impact would surely kill them. But the train righted itself and tipped the other way, crashing onto the tracks. Darrion and Ryan still clung to the metal pole in midair as glass smashed and people screamed.

Judd told Mr. Stahley to find Diversey. They kept the L tracks in sight as they flew through the city.

"This is what I was afraid of," Mr. Stahley said. "They've triggered the second attack on Chicago just as the potentate planned."

Judd noticed the attack seemed concentrated to his left toward the lakeshore. It looked like Michigan Avenue, known as the Magnificent Mile, was under heavy bombing.

Mr. Stahley stopped only at intersections where emergency vehicles were passing. Otherwise he honked his horn and ran through stop signs and red lights. A bicycle messenger darted out in front of the car, and Mr. Stahley swerved to avoid a head-on collision.

"The world's at war and you still have to dodge those guys," Mr. Stahley said.

Cars were abandoned in the middle of the road while people sought some kind of shelter. But where the bombs landed, there was no shelter. Smoke and flames rose into the air as they drove.

They passed an L stop, and Vicki screamed. "A white van! We must be close."

Mr. Stahley floored the accelerator and sped down a street parallel to the tracks. He jumped the curb and barreled through an alley, winding through a maze of trash cans and parked cars.

Mr. Stahley slammed on his brakes and cursed. Judd looked up and saw a horrifying sight. Before them was the L track with a huge hole in one section. At the edge of the flames, a train sat on its side, as if some giant had pushed it over. People were scrambling to get out of windows.

"Do you think that's the one?" Vicki said.

"It has to be," Judd said.

Darrion pulled herself up on the pole and grabbed Ryan's hand. "All that work on the uneven parallel bars finally paid off," Darrion said. "Now what do we do?"

Ryan reached for the door, but he was short a few inches.

"Here, son," a man below him said. "Use this."

The man handed him an umbrella. Ryan stuck it into the soft rubber between the doors and jabbed at it. Nothing happened. Darrion pointed to an emergency button beside the door. When he hit it with the umbrella, the door popped open.

The two stood on top of the train and tried to get their balance. They could see into apartment buildings and the burning city around them. People were trying to crawl on top of the train. Some made it and spilled onto the tracks. Smoke and debris spread through the area, making it difficult to see.

"Please remain inside the train car," the conductor said through the scratchy speakers. "Do not walk on the tracks. The rail is electrified. You are in danger."

"As soon as we get on the ground and away from those goons," Ryan said, "I want to pray with you."

"Sounds like a plan," Darrion said.

When they came to the end of the first car, Darrion and Ryan jumped and landed safely on top of the second car. When they reached the caboose, Ryan took Darrion's hand and dropped her gently to the tracks.

"Wait for me," Ryan called down to her. "I don't want you to get close to the third rail."

Another bomb fell close to the tracks, and Ryan braced himself. The tracks swayed but didn't buckle. He regained his balance and was surprised to see Darrion running away through a cloud of smoke.

Ryan jumped to the tracks. Darrion was headed back to the station. He was about to scream at her to stop when two men passed him. Carl and the short man.

We're too close to let them catch us now, he thought. As Ryan took off, he noticed something strange underneath the tracks. A silver car drove wildly, honking its horn and racing toward the station.

"Judd!" Ryan said.

NINE

One More Hurdle

VICKI felt vibration in the backseat as the Mercedes clattered underneath the tracks. The muffler had come loose and was banging the ground.

"There she is!" Judd shouted, pointing overhead. "She's going back the other way."

Mr. Stahley whipped the steering wheel to the left and slammed on his brakes. The car spun perfectly, kicking dust into the air, then was pointed in the right direction.

Something on the instrument panel of the car beeped, but neither Mr. Stahley nor Judd paid it any attention. Vicki craned her neck and saw Darrion sprinting down the tracks. She was small but very fast.

The Mercedes was a block away from the train stop when Vicki saw a flash of head-lights to her left. She braced herself for impact and screamed a warning as a car blindsided them, sending the Mercedes into a chain-link fence.

Vicki was stunned. Judd and Mr. Stahley struggled to release their seat belts.

"Everybody okay?" Mr. Stahley said.

Vicki and Judd nodded. The driver's side door was smashed, so the three climbed out Judd's side. When they were finally out, a voice behind them said, "Hold it right there."

Vicki glanced at the other car and recognized it from the expressway.

So that's why the light was beeping, Vicki thought.

Ryan ran behind the men a few paces. He was careful to stay in the middle of the track and keep his balance. Darrion was almost to the platform now.

He heard a crash of metal underneath the tracks. The silver car was against a fence. One of the men in the other car jumped out. He had a gun.

Ryan looked up and saw Darrion struggling to climb onto the wooden platform. The men following Ryan were closing in when someone in a trench coat reached out and helped her up.

"All right!" Ryan shouted.

But the man didn't let go. He held Darrion

by her elbow and roughly dragged her to the stairs. The men in front of him stopped and turned.

"No!" Ryan screamed.

"Get him," Carl said.

Vicki saw the gun and put up her hands. The man motioned for the three of them to move beside a concrete slab underneath the tracks.

"Where's your boss?" Mr. Stahley said.

"That's none of your concern," the man said. He had short hair and wore a long, black coat. "You should have stayed home."

"And leave my daughter to the likes of you—"

"Your daughter would have been returned," the man said.

"And how long would it have taken to send a guided missile into my living room?"

The man with the gun smiled and put his finger to his lips. "Time for talking's over," he said. "I have my orders."

"Your orders didn't say anything about them," Mr. Stahley said, nodding toward Judd and Vicki. "They're innocent."

The man looked at the two teenagers. "Sorry," he said. "They know too much."

Ryan was better at running the tracks than the men. The short man was red in the face and puffing behind Carl. A hundred yards ahead the train lay on its side, and beyond that the burning tracks. Ryan knew he had to act fast. As he went past the silver car below and saw the man with the gun, he caught sight of a metal ladder built onto the track. He would have to cross the electrified rail to get to it, but if he could reach it before his captors, he could make it to the ground.

It killed him not to go after Darrion. But what good would he be if he were caught? He looked back to the platform once, but Darrion was gone. Then he spotted the man with the trench coat below the tracks. He still had Darrion by the arm.

Judd saw a man holding a young girl by the arm.

"Darrion!" Mr. Stahley cried.

The man in the trench coat threw the girl into the other car. He looked at Mr. Stahley. "Take care of him," the man snapped.

"Yes, sir," the man in the black coat said.

The car sped away. Judd held Mr. Stahley's arm. They had only one chance now.

Ryan met a group slowly making its way from the train. He dodged them, then quickly jumped the third rail and grabbed the rungs of the ladder. A woman in the group screamed. The short man had a gun. He leveled it at Ryan.

Suddenly, a huge explosion sent the entire group to the tracks. Ryan held on to the ladder with all his might. When the vibrations stopped, Ryan saw that the two men had fallen on the electrified third rail.

Judd fell to the ground at the explosion. Mr. Stahley rushed the man with the gun. Before he could reach him, the man had regained his balance and pulled himself up by the concrete support.

Judd noticed movement overhead. Someone was climbing down the side of the tracks.

Ryan!

Judd looked away and coughed. He caught Vicki's eye.

"We don't really know what this is about," Judd said, walking a few paces.

"Stay where you are," the man with the gun said, turning slightly as Ryan climbed down the ladder behind him.

"It's not fair," Vicki said, putting a hand over her eyes. "We're just kids. We didn't know!" She wept bitterly. Only Judd knew it was an act.

Ryan slowed until the man with the gun moved slightly. Vicki was crying. That would cover the noise of his descent.

Ryan stepped onto a ledge about ten feet above the ground. He knew he wasn't big enough to wrestle the gun from the man, but if he jumped him, Ryan guessed the surprise and the weight of his fall would give Judd, Vicki, and the other man the chance they needed.

Ryan's feet landed squarely on the man's shoulders, and they both tumbled to the ground. Judd put his foot on the man's wrist, and the gun fired. Mr. Stahley wrestled the gun from him.

"Ryan Daley, meet Maxwell Stahley," Judd said as they subdued the gunman.

"Darrion's dad?" Ryan said.

"I am," Mr. Stahley said. He held the gun on the man while Judd looked for something to bind him.

"Sure is good to see you," Vicki said. "Lionel wouldn't let us give up."

"Can't wait to see him," Ryan said. "Bruce too."

Judd and Mr. Stahley tied the man with some rope Judd found in the Mercedes. They opened the damaged trunk, shoved the man in, and shut the lid.

The car was sluggish when they pulled away. A huge pool of antifreeze was on the ground. As they drove, Ryan quickly explained what he had heard the two men say about moving Darrion. "They said something about taking her to sector four, whatever that means," he said.

"Sector four is the northern quadrant of Chicago," Mr. Stahley said. "The Global Community has different security offices in each quadrant."

"So you know where the place is?" Ryan said.

"It could be any one of a dozen I can think of," Mr. Stahley said calmly.

A cell phone rang. It took Ryan a few seconds to realize it was in his back pocket. "This could be the boss guy," Ryan said.

"Don't answer it," Mr. Stahley said.

"But how are we going to know how to find Darrion?" Ryan said.

Mr. Stahley pointed to the screen in the dashboard.

"The tracking device!" Vicki said.

"Cool," Ryan said as he watched Mr. Stahley weave in and out of traffic. Cars coming into the city were at a standstill. Emergency vehicles tried to get near the injured.

"We have to find her," Ryan said. "We talked a lot about God, and she said she was ready."

Mr. Stahley was quiet as Judd and Vicki asked Ryan questions about what he and Darrion had discussed. When they were on the expressway, Mr. Stahley turned on the radio.

"It's not clear whether this attack on Chicago was nuclear," the reporter said.

"If it had been nuclear," Mr. Stahley said, "the radiation would've gotten us by now."

". . . and in just a moment we understand we will go live to the potentate," the reporter continued. "Recapping our top story, a massive attack on Chicago has leveled much of Michigan Avenue. Thousands are feared dead. . . ."

Ryan gave a low whistle. "That could have been us," he said.

"Ladies and gentlemen," the reporter said, "from an unknown location, we bring you live, Global Community Potentate Nicolae Carpathia."

There was a slight pause.

"He's probably in a plane somewhere," Mr. Stahley said. "He'll use his most emotional voice."

"Brothers and sisters of the Global Community," Carpathia said. "I am speaking to you with the greatest heaviness of heart I have ever known. I am a man of peace who has been forced to retaliate with arms against international terrorists. You may rest assured that I grieve with you over the loss of loved ones, of friends, of acquaintances. The horrible toll of civilian lives should haunt these enemies of peace for the rest of their days.

"As you know, most of the ten world regions that comprise the Global Community destroyed 90 percent of their weapon hardware. We have spent nearly the last two years breaking down, packaging, shipping, receiving, and reassembling this hardware in New Babylon. My humble prayer was that we would never have had to use it.

"However, wise counselors persuaded me to stockpile these weapons in strategic locations around the globe. I confess I did this against my will. Now it appears that decision was a good one.

"In my wildest dreams, I never would have imagined that I would have to turn this power against enemies on a broad scale."

Carpathia talked about two members of his inner circle who had conspired against him, and another who had carelessly allowed

militia forces in his region to do the same.
"The forces were led by the now late presi-
dent of the United States of North America,
Gerald Fitzhugh," Carpathia said.

"Did he say the 'late' Gerald Fitzhugh?"
Vicki said.

"They wouldn't allow that man to live any
more than they want to let me live," Mr.
Stahley said.

"I thought you said you were just raising
concerns about the air strikes," Judd said.
"Couldn't you go back and say you'd made a
mistake?"

"I could try," Mr. Stahley said, "but I don't
think it would do any good. Now that the
attack has been successful, my fate is sealed.
There is no reason for them to allow me to
live. I only hope I can get my wife and daughter to safety before they accomplish their goal."

Carpathia was still going. "While I should
never have to defend my reputation as an
antiwar activist, I am pleased to inform you
that we have retaliated severely and with
dispatch. Anywhere that Global Community
weaponry was used, it was aimed specifically
at rebel military locations. I assure you that
all casualties were the work of the rebellion."

"Is that true?" Ryan said. "Those were militia planes today?"

"Of course not," Mr. Stahley said, "but

everyone will buy it because they want to believe in Carpathia."

"There are no more plans for counterattacks by Global Community forces," Carpathia continued. "We will respond only as necessary and pray that our enemies understand that they have no future. They cannot succeed. They will be destroyed.

"I know that in a time of global war such as this, most of us live in fear and grief. I can assure you that I am with you in your grief but that my fear has been overcome by confidence that the majority of the global community is together, heart and soul, against the enemies of peace.

"As soon as I am convinced of security and safety, I will address you via satellite television and the Internet. I will communicate frequently so you know exactly what is going on and will see that we are making enormous strides toward rebuilding our world. You may rest assured that as we reconstruct and reorganize, we will enjoy the greatest prosperity and the most wonderful home this earth can afford. May we all work together for the common goal."

Judd thought of Rabbi Ben-Judah, his wife and children. They might be on their way to

America at that very moment. Their situation paralleled the Stahleys, but for different reasons. The Stahleys were a risk to Nicolae for political and security reasons. The Ben-Judahs were at risk because of their faith.

Judd was exhausted. He helped Mr. Stahley follow the transmitter until they drove up beside what looked like a ritzy office complex. The building was made of granite. The top of the building was smaller than the base, and the polished sides sloped down.

"There it is!" Vicki said as they rounded the corner. A car with a smashed front fender was parked askew at the back entrance to the building.

"What's the plan?" Judd said.

"I'll get into the building alone with my security card," Mr. Stahley said.

"No way," Ryan said. "I'm going too."

"We'll need someone who can drive to keep the car running," Mr. Stahley said. "Judd, that means you. We also need someone at the front in case Darrion gets free."

"I can do that," Vicki said.

"And in case something happens to me, Ryan, you stand inside the back door. I'll call if I need help. It's the best plan."

"It could be a trap," Ryan said. "If that guy

can't reach his friend in the trunk, they'll suspect you're coming, right?"

"I'll take that chance," Mr. Stahley said. "My one goal is to get Darrion out of there alive. Outside of that, I don't care."

Mr. Stahley took the gun he had taken from the man in the trunk. Vicki ran to the front of the building. Judd stayed behind the wheel.

"Stay here and listen," Mr. Stahley said to Ryan. "And I need something else. It's very important."

"Whatever you say," Ryan said as they entered the building.

"Pray," Mr. Stahley said.

Vicki stole to the front of the building and tried to look in the windows. The glass was so clean she could see her reflection in the dim moonlight. In the distance she could see the city of Chicago in flames.

She moved away from the building a few paces and noticed a light on the fifth floor. It was the only light on in the building.

Judd fidgeted and turned on the radio. He heard more news of global devastation. World War III was raging. He hadn't heard the man in the trunk for a while. The man had thumped and kicked throughout the ride. Now he wondered if the guy had been overcome by fumes.

He took the key from the ignition and went to the back of the car. He knocked on the trunk. "You okay in there?" Judd said.

No answer.

Judd put the key in and turned it till it clicked. Suddenly the trunk burst open, and the man who had been bound was on Judd. Judd struggled, but the man was bigger and stronger.

"Where's Stahley?" the man yelled as he held Judd down.

"Ryan, help!" Judd yelled. The man was after the car key. Judd kept struggling, but the man had Judd's hand and was prying it open.

A shot rang out inside the building, and the man leaped to his feet. Then another shot, and another. Judd jumped in the car and locked the doors. The man ran toward the building. Judd honked the horn, hoping Ryan would lock the back door.

Vicki backed up on the lawn to get a better look at the building. Suddenly the curtain pulled back. It was Darrion. Mr. Stahley stood behind her. He raised his gun and shot at the glass. The window didn't break. He shot again and again. Then he threw himself against the window. It cracked slightly but didn't give way.

Then she heard a horn honk. She ran to the back and was nearly knocked over by the man in the black coat, who sprinted toward the roadway. The last time she saw him, he was flagging down a car on the access road to the building.

As soon as Ryan heard the gunfire, he bolted up the stairs. The door closed behind him. Ryan stopped at each landing to listen. When he got to the fifth floor he heard a voice. He gingerly opened the stairwell door and stepped inside the hallway.

Ryan stayed a safe distance away and kept quiet. The man in the trench coat was down the hall talking to someone through a closed door.

"It's no use," the man said. "The glass is unbreakable. I have you both."

"You've failed," Mr. Stahley said from inside the room. His voice was muffled, but Ryan could make out his words.

"And how have I failed?" the man said.

"My laptop," Mr. Stahley said. "If I don't disable it in the next five minutes, an E-mail is sent to every news organization in North

America. I'm sure the information is something Mr. Carpathia would not want disseminated."

"Where is the computer?" the man said flatly.

"Release my daughter and I'll take you to it," Mr. Stahley said.

Ryan heard a huge crash of glass downstairs. The man quickly turned the key to unlock the room. Now there were footsteps on the stairs behind him. He stepped inside a doorway and watched Judd bolt through the stairwell door, with Vicki right behind. The man in the trench coat turned and fired. Judd hit the floor and rolled toward Ryan. Vicki stopped just inside the stairwell.

The door to the room flew open, and Mr. Stahley faced his enemy. The men were only two feet apart when they both fired and fell to the ground. Judd, Vicki, and Ryan ran to Mr. Stahley's side.

"Take the gun out of his hand," Mr. Stahley gasped.

Ryan pulled the gun from the other man's hand, but he could tell there was no reason to fear. The other man was dead.

Darrion knelt over her father. "Dad, are you gonna be okay?"

"I don't know, honey. I'm just glad you're safe."

There was blood on Mr. Stahley's shirt. "We need to get you to the hospital," Darrion said.

"Wait," Mr. Stahley said, grabbing his daughter's arm. "Ryan told us what you talked about. He said you've made a decision. About God."

"Yeah," Darrion said. "I'm sorry, Daddy, but I think Aunt Linda and Uncle Ken were right. I think—"

Mr. Stahley interrupted her. "I believe they were, too, honey. I was blind to the truth."

Darrion looked at Ryan. "How do we do it?" she said. "What do we say?"

Ryan took a breath.

"The Bible says if you confess with your mouth that Jesus is Lord and believe in your heart that God raised him from the dead, you will be saved. Just pray something like this. God, I know I've sinned. I'm sorry."

As Ryan prayed, Darrion prayed out loud. Ryan watched Mr. Stahley's lips move as well.

"Right now I confess I believe you died for me on the cross. I accept your forgiveness for my sin and I put all my hope and trust in

you. Come into my heart right now, in Jesus'
name. Amen."

Vicki and Judd both said, "Amen."

Darrion opened her eyes and smiled at
Ryan. Mr. Stahley was silent.

"Daddy?" Darrion cried. "Daddy!"

TEN

Home

RYAN knew they had to leave Mr. Stahley and get to safety. When Judd crashed the car through the back door, an alarm would go off somewhere. If they hung around, no telling who might show up. Plus, knowing Mr. Stahley was dead might satisfy others in the Global Community who wanted the rest of the family dead.

Darrion was overcome with grief. Ryan held her arm as she walked down the stairs.

"What about the laptop?" Ryan said to Judd, explaining what Mr. Stahley had said.

"It had to be a ruse," Judd said. "Mr. Stahley didn't have a laptop with him."

"This car won't make it much farther," Vicki said when they made it to the Mercedes.

"We only need to get to the forest

preserve," Judd said. "We'll pick up my car and—"

"My mother!" Darrion cried as they pulled out. "We have to get my mother. They'll come for her."

Vicki dialed the number Darrion gave. Twenty minutes later they met Mrs. Stahley at the stable where Darrion had been abducted. The two embraced and wept bitterly. Judd and Ryan drove to the forest preserve. They scoured the car to remove any clues of their identity. Judd drove them all to Mt. Prospect.

It was dark when they pulled into Judd's driveway. Lionel rushed out to greet Ryan. The kids helped Mrs. Stahley and Darrion inside. When Darrion was able to speak, she talked about the decision she and her father had made.

"You should have seen his face, Mom," Darrion said. "He seemed at peace. All those things we said, the way we ridiculed Aunt Linda and Uncle Ken for what they believed. They were right. We missed the truth."

"I want to thank you for saving my daughter's life," Mrs. Stahley said to Ryan. "I don't know what to say."

Darrion turned to Ryan. "Where is he now?" she said. "Does my dad's soul go to heaven, or does that happen some other time?"

"I asked Bruce that same question," Ryan said. "The Bible is clear. When a Christian dies, he or she goes to be with God. That means there's a big reunion going on right now with your father and your other family members who were Christians."

"That's comforting," Darrion said. Then she turned to her mother. "Mom, are you ready to listen?"

"Not just yet," Mrs. Stahley said.

"He would want you to," Darrion said.

Mrs. Stahley wiped her eyes and turned to Ryan. "Then tell me what you told my daughter and my husband." she said.

Ryan opened a Bible and let Mrs. Stahley read the verses he had quoted to Darrion earlier. Mrs. Stahley wept more when Ryan explained the depth of God's love. "Even though we're sinful," Ryan said, "Christ died so that we might live with him."

Mrs. Stahley asked questions and stared at the Bible. Finally she took Darrion's hand. "I knew in my heart there was something to what Ken and Linda were saying," she said. "But I didn't want to believe it. Now I know it's true. Whatever time I have left on this earth, I want God to have control. I want him to use me in some way."

Judd and Vicki prayed with Darrion and Mrs. Stahley, then took them downstairs to Vicki's old room. They would spend the night at Judd's, then move to a safer location.

Judd walked to Ryan's room and asked if they could talk about something important.

"Sure," Ryan said. "Hey, I told you I'd get to see Bruce. Didn't think I could even get in, but I did."

"I'm glad you did," Judd said. "It must have been something, getting through all those people at the hospital without being seen."

"Wasn't that hard," Ryan said humbly. "What did you want to tell me?"

Judd wished he didn't have to tell Ryan the bad news, but he knew he couldn't keep it from him any longer. If they did survive the next few years before the return of Christ, there would be more bad news.

"Ryan," Judd said, "you took a bunch of chances today, and it seems God used you. Part of me wants to scold you for taking off and not telling us. But I have to say I'm really proud of the way you trusted God."

"I'd be lying if I said I wasn't scared," Ryan

said. "Especially when those guys kept talking about dropping me in the water."

"You didn't let your fears keep you from doing what was right. You put your life on the line for somebody else. I know that kind of sacrifice pleases God."

"Yeah, Bruce always said God can do big things through you when you feel the weakest. That way he gets the glory."

Judd thought hard. *How can you tell someone their best friend is gone?*

"So, when can I call Bruce?" Ryan said. "You guys didn't tell him anything about me being gone, did you? I wouldn't want him to have a relapse or whatever you call it."

Judd bit his lip. "Ryan, God has one more thing he wants you to trust him with."

"Hey, you don't have to be dramatic," Ryan said. "Just tell me."

"Do you remember this morning when you left the hospital? You heard all the explosions, right?"

"You bet. Smoke was everywhere. I didn't think I'd make it out alive."

"The target was the Nike base. It was a militia outpost. A lot of people were killed in there—"

"Is it Mark?" Ryan said gravely. "Was he at that Nike base thing?"

"He was there," Judd said, "but they sent him out before it was bombed. He's okay, but still a little shaky."

"Then what's the deal? Tell me. I can take it."

"Ryan, one of the first bombs fell on the hospital. The only survivors of the blast were outside when the bombs hit."

Ryan's eyes looked vacant. "It's about Bruce, isn't it?" he said.

"Yeah."

Ryan shook Judd's arm loose and stood. "Are you sure? I mean, couldn't he be under the rubble somewhere? I've heard of people in buildings like that who live for a week."

"Ryan—"

"Come on," Ryan said as he pulled Judd's arm, "we have to go back and make sure."

Judd stood and grabbed Ryan's shoulders. He looked Ryan square in the face, knowing what he was about to say would crush the boy. "We're not going back," Judd said. "There's no point. Bruce is dead."

Ryan narrowed his eyes. "How do you know if you don't even try!" he said through clenched teeth. "How can you just give up on him like that, after all he's done for you?"

"I saw him," Judd said. He was emotional but controlled. "I pulled the sheet back from his face."

Ryan turned away and looked out the window. He ran for the bedroom door, but Judd grabbed him.

"I don't want to hurt you," Judd said tenderly. "I'd do anything if I could bring him back, but I can't. It tore my heart out to see him like that, and to have to tell you is just as hard. But we have to face the truth."

Ryan fell onto the bed and put his arm over his face.

"It's gonna be hard," Judd said, "but we'll get through this together."

"Leave me alone," Ryan said.

"Come into the other room with us," Judd said.

"I want to be alone," Ryan repeated. He didn't seem angry. "It's okay. I just want to think a little."

A thousand thoughts flashed through Ryan's head. In the terror and excitement of the day, with his goal of staying alive and telling Darrion about the love of God, he hadn't thought much about Bruce possibly being hurt. Now Bruce was dead.

Dead. *What does it mean?*

Ryan had been able to talk with Bruce like with no one else. He hadn't even talked with his mom or dad like that. Bruce listened. He cared. When Lionel got on his nerves or Judd bossed him around, Ryan could go to Bruce. Even when Bruce was on a trip, he took time to e-mail and always brought back some kind of souvenir.

Then Ryan thought of Israel, and the tears came. Bruce had promised to take him. Ryan had tried to make Bruce feel bad about passing him by, and now he felt empty. He'd heard Judd and Bruce talk about the things they'd seen on their trips. He'd looked the different sites up on the Internet and had even done reports for religion class. Now he'd never get to go.

What about the Bible room? the church?

There were thousands of people around the world who depended on Bruce and his teaching. Why would God take a man so totally committed, so sold out to the cause of Christ? Who could God provide to take his place?

Ryan brought back the last moments he had spent with Bruce in the hospital. He had opened the card that looked like heaven and held it in front of Bruce's closed eyes. And then a wonderful thing had happened. Bruce had raised his hand and placed it on Ryan's shoulder. A tear ran down Bruce's cheek as they said good-bye. *Somehow, Bruce must have known,* Ryan thought.

Through the sadness and the feeling of loss, Ryan thought of something that made him smile. Bruce taught him that no matter how bad things seem, if God was in control, there was always something good to think about. The thought came when Ryan remembered the pictures in his Bible room. Bruce had given Ryan a treasured photo of his family. Ryan closed his eyes and saw it. Bruce and his wife. His two older children beside him and the little baby on his wife's lap. Ryan knew Bruce didn't have to grieve for his family any longer. Bruce was with his wife. He could see his children and talk with them.

Ryan had brought up the subject of heaven numerous times in their studies. He knew heaven was a real place. He knew people would recognize each other there. He knew he would have a different type of body, one that wouldn't get sick or die. People who were blind or couldn't walk wouldn't have those problems anymore. He tried to picture the moment when Bruce saw his family again.

Then a thought overwhelmed Ryan. He sat up on the bed. Bruce was now in the presence of the person he loved most and who loved him. Jesus. For some reason God had allowed Bruce to die, and even though Ryan couldn't understand it, the thought of Bruce face-to-face with Jesus made the tears pour. But they weren't tears of grief.

"God," Ryan prayed, "I do trust you. I believe you can help me get through this. Thanks for bringing me home. Thanks for answering my prayers about Darrion. Thanks for my friends. Help me get over Bruce's death. And tell him I said I'll miss him. Amen."

Before Ryan stood, he heard a scratching at the door. When he opened it, Phoenix bounded in and bowled him over, licking his face and smothering him with affection.

Judd wanted to check on Ryan, but Vicki shook her head. "He needs the time," she said. "You did a good job in there."

"How do you know I did a good job?" Judd said.

Vicki squirmed. "I kind of listened at the door."

Judd took Vicki in the kitchen to talk alone. "We can't keep Darrion and Mrs. Stahley here," he said. "In fact, I don't think any of us can stay. The Global Community guys have our number. They could follow the trail right here."

"We could take them to Bruce's house,"

Vicki said. "There's plenty of room with Bruce gone. . . ." Vicki's voice trailed. She looked up with teary eyes. "What are we going to do, Judd? Bruce was like a parent to all of us."

"I've been thinking a lot about that," Judd said. "The Young Tribulation Force is going to grow. Our money's gone. We can't stay here and don't have the time to sell the place. And we've got company coming." Judd explained that the Ben-Judah family was coming to live with them.

"I wish we could solve all this like they do on TV," Vicki said. "Just hire a nanny or something. Everything works out in thirty minutes."

Judd lifted her chin with his hand. "Can I tell you something?" he said. "The way you acted today," Judd said, "the way you faced danger and didn't give up. I really admire how strong you are. How resourceful you've become."

"Thank you," Vicki said, blushing. "I've always thought we made a pretty good team."

The doorbell rang. Judd checked before he opened the door and was surprised to see Chaya.

"Thank God you're all right," Chaya said.

Darrion and Mrs. Stahley came back upstairs. Chaya explained how she had been able to help decipher Ryan's clue on the phone.

Mrs. Stahley raised a hand. "My daughter and I face an uncertain future without my husband," she said. "I'm not sure how this is supposed to work, but I suddenly feel as if I'm needed."

Judd didn't understand what the woman was trying to say. "We're here for *you*, ma'am," Judd said. "We're going to take care of you."

"And I thank you," she said. "But I feel as if I should offer something. Not as a reward, but as a fellow family member."

"What are you saying?" Vicki said.

"As you and Judd know, our family has no lack of resources. It could very well be that the Global Community will freeze our bank assets. But I want you to know the money, the cars, the land, all we have I want to share. I will withdraw our money as quickly as possible so it can be used for a good purpose. I know Maxwell would agree with me."

Judd was stunned. "We have huge financial needs," he said. "But you can't—"

"It's already been decided," Mrs. Stahley said. "I said I wanted God to use me, and this is just a small way to do that." Mrs. Stahley asked to use a computer to transfer funds from her account. "If I wait, it may be too late."

Judd showed her the computer in his father's office. Within a few minutes she had successfully transferred funds to Judd's account and another secret account in another country.

"Now we must rest," Mrs. Stahley said, taking Darrion downstairs.

Vicki looked at Judd. "Can you believe it?" she said.

"I'm still trying to take it in," Judd said.

"I don't mean to be the bearer of more bad news," Chaya said, "but I'm afraid some things are getting worse. Have you heard anything from Buck Williams?"

"No," Judd said, "the last time I saw him he was headed to *Global Community Weekly.*"

"That's where he went," Chaya said. "I just got off the phone with Loretta, who filled me in. Chloe dropped Buck off at the office, then went downtown to get their stuff out of The Drake Hotel. They were planning to stay with Loretta tonight. But when Chloe got to the hotel, she took a message from her dad. He said they should get out of Chicago as fast as they could."

"Captain Steele must have found out

about the bombing," Judd said. "Did she get out?"

"Buck was on the cell phone with her when the first bombs hit," Chaya said. "She was on Lake Shore Drive."

"Oh no," Vicki said. "Lake Shore is really close to Michigan Avenue, where most of the damage was done."

"Where's Buck now?" Judd said.

"He borrowed a car from somebody he works with, and now he's headed downtown to see if he can find Chloe," Chaya said.

"When we came from there it looked pretty hopeless," Judd said. "Traffic was a mess. I can't imagine what it's like now."

Judd grabbed his jacket and asked Vicki and Chaya to spend the night at his house. "I'll call you as soon as I find out anything," he said.

Judd flipped on the radio as he drove toward Loretta's. The reporters confirmed Mr. Stahley's fears. Chicago wasn't the only target.

"We've just received confirmation of the attack on San Francisco," the announcer said. "It's impossible to estimate the number of dead at this point, but airports and other transportation centers have been destroyed."

Judd shuddered. He recalled the news of the devastating attack on Heathrow Airport in London. The main centers of transportation were being bombed. Communication centers. Trade centers. This would allow Carpathia to have a stranglehold on the world's economy, transportation, and communication.

A coworker of Buck's, Verna Zee, met Judd at Loretta's door and let him in. Loretta was on the phone with Buck. Verna looked distraught.

"Here, Verna," Loretta said, "Buck wants to talk to you."

Verna took the phone. "Oh no, Cameron," she said, "what happened?"

Loretta told Judd that Buck was somewhere near Lake Shore Drive in Chicago but hadn't found Chloe. "Buck showed up with Verna a while ago, and I opened my home to her," she said. "She seems like a nice person, but confused. I've just been tellin' her my story."

Verna got off the phone. "He wrecked my car," she said. "Said he'd replace it with a better one. Can't argue with that. He's close to Michigan Avenue. I'm not sure he's going to find anything tonight."

Verna dialed the newsroom and talked with a staff member. She thanked the man and told him to call if there were any more messages.

"Buck got three calls," Verna told Judd, "but none from his wife."

The phone rang. It was Buck.

"No," Verna told Buck, "but you did get a call from a Dr. Rosenzweig in Israel, and another was from a man claiming to be your father-in-law."

Judd blocked out the rest of the conversation. Loretta offered him something to drink, but he couldn't concentrate. The name of Chaim Rosenzweig made him think of Dr. Tsion Ben-Judah. Dr. Rosenzweig was a mentor to the rabbi. Judd thought about Ben-Judah's children, Nina and Dan, and their mother. He prayed they would be safe and able to make it to Chicago.

From the living room, Judd heard the phone ring again. This time Verna let out a whoop. She hung up and dialed another number.

"No, Cameron, it's Verna," Judd heard her say, "but the office just called. Chloe just tried to reach you. She didn't say where she was or how she was, but at least you know she's alive."

Judd put his head down on the couch for a moment. Since the night of the disappearances, it had been the most tumultuous day of his life. He had lost a dear friend. He had seen Darrion, her mother, and her father accept the gift of salvation. He had witnessed Mr. Stahley's death and the deaths of others. He had seen destruction near his home and in downtown Chicago. In the midst of it all, he had seen the power of God's love at work in the lives of his friends.

Judd closed his eyes only for a moment. When he opened them, light streamed through the window, and he heard familiar voices of the people he loved.

ABOUT THE AUTHORS

Jerry B. Jenkins (www.jerryjenkins.com) is the writer of the Left Behind series. He is author of more than one hundred books, of which eleven have reached the *New York Times* best-seller list. Former vice president for publishing for the Moody Bible Institute of Chicago, he also served many years as editor of *Moody* magazine and is now Moody's writer-at-large.

His writing has appeared in publications as varied as *Reader's Digest, Parade,* in-flight magazines, and many Christian periodicals. He has written books in four genres: biography, marriage and family, fiction for children, and fiction for adults.

Jenkins's biographies include books with Hank Aaron, Bill Gaither, Luis Palau, Walter Payton, Orel Hershiser, Nolan Ryan, Brett Butler, and Billy Graham, among many others.

Eight of his apocalyptic novels—*Left Behind, Tribulation Force, Nicolae, Soul Harvest, Apollyon, Assassins, The Indwelling,* and *The Mark*—have appeared on the Christian Booksellers Association's best-selling fiction list and the *Publishers Weekly* religion best-seller list. *Left Behind* was nominated for Book of the Year by the Evangelical Christian Publishers Association in 1997, 1998, 1999, and 2000. *The Indwelling* was number one on the *New York Times* best-seller list for four consecutive weeks.

As a marriage and family author and speaker, Jenkins has been a frequent guest on Dr. James Dobson's *Focus on the Family* radio program.

Jerry is also the writer of the nationally syndicated sports story comic strip *Gil Thorp,* distributed to newspapers across the United States by Tribune Media Services.

Jerry and his wife, Dianna, live in Colorado.

Dr. Tim LaHaye (www.timlahaye.com), who conceived the idea of fictionalizing an account of the Rapture and the Tribulation, is a noted author, minister, and nationally recognized speaker on Bible prophecy. He is the founder of both Tim LaHaye Ministries and The Pre-Trib Research Center. Presently Dr. LaHaye speaks at many of the major Bible prophecy conferences in the U.S. and Canada, where his nine current prophecy books are very popular.

Dr. LaHaye holds a doctor of ministry degree from Western Theological Seminary and the doctor of literature degree from Liberty University. For twenty-five years he pastored one of the nation's outstanding churches in San Diego, which grew to three locations. It was during that time that he founded two accredited Christian high schools, a Christian school system of ten schools, and Christian Heritage College.

Dr. LaHaye has written over forty books, with over 30 million copies in print in thirty-three languages. He has written books on a wide variety of subjects, such as family life, temperaments, and Bible prophecy. His current fiction works, written with Jerry Jenkins—*Left Behind, Tribulation Force, Nicolae, Soul Harvest, Apollyon, Assassins, The Indwelling,* and *The Mark*—have all reached number one on the Christian best-seller charts. Other works by Dr. LaHaye are *Spirit-Controlled Temperament; How to Be Happy Though Married; Revelation Unveiled; Understanding the Last Days; Rapture under Attack; Are We Living in the End Times?;* and the youth fiction series Left Behind: The Kids.

He is the father of four grown children and grand-father of nine. Snow skiing, waterskiing, motorcycling, golfing, vacationing with family, and jogging are among his leisure activities.

The Future Is Clear

Check out the exciting Left Behind: The Kids series

Books #19 and #20 coming soon!

Discover the latest about the Left Behind series and complete line of products at

www.leftbehind.com